Decoded Desires

B. Lynn Hedge

First edition

This book is for all of the wonderful people who took a chance on me as a new author.

I can never thank you all enough for your love and support throughout this process, and I'm so glad to have you back!

Also, a special shoutout to my family, for all of your continued support as I set out to achieve more than I thought I ever would.

Love you lots..

Contents

Foreword

This is a continuation of the Golden Locke Series. Encrypted Emotions must be read before this book to make sense of it.

Lottie is a character who was previously described as having Asperger's. Although this is an outdated diagnosis no longer used, it is what the character believes is correct. It is addressed and discussed in the book.

This book, while spicier than the last… it is still a slow-burn romance as we watch Lottie's relationships grow.

This book centers around a main character who is on the spectrum, and with that, there are also mentions of anxiety and panic attacks.

The book also contains mentions of sex trafficking, kidnapping, mental health, violence, and self-deprecation.

This is a reverse harem romance, meaning our main character, Charlotte, is in a relationship with multiple men.

If you are alright with all of the above, then please proceed and enjoy the next installment of Charlotte's journey.

1

~ Cooper ~

"Kai, would you please stop pacing. You're making me nauseous." I beg my hyperactive brother from across the waiting room as he turns to cross the space again.

It's been 4 hours.

No answers.

Just waiting.

Yesterday had been amazing, all of us together and our usual family traditions, but this time with Charlotte making everything brighter. Having her with us brought back that childhood excitement; it was a truly perfect day.

And then I got the call.

I'd been so confused when my phone woke me up this morning, especially seeing Mav's name light up the screen. He had been in his office last night after we opened gifts, so the fact that he was calling me stirred up my confusion, only to be paired with concern when I looked around the living room to find that Charlotte was no longer lying on the couch between us.

Hearing his voice through the phone had me on high alert in an instant. I'd woken Kai and Eli and rushed us to the hospital to wait for an update.

Maverick had only been here for half an hour when he called, which meant we were coming up on 4 hours without hearing from any of the doctors. My nerves are shot; I can't take much more of not knowing what's going on. And I really can't take any more of Kai's pacing.

He must be able to see how close I am to losing it, because he lets out a frustrated breath before sinking into the seat next to Eli, who has not said a word since I woke him this morning and has been staring at a scuff on the floor ever since he sat down.

I am, however, surprised at Maverick's reaction to all of this. He'd sounded frantic when he called, which is understandable given how he found Charlotte. But from the moment we got here, he's been buzzing with anxious energy, fidgeting with his phone, or tugging at his hair; I'm afraid he's going to rip it out. If I didn't know any better, I'd say he looks distraught, which is interesting with how much he pretends not to care about Charlotte.

"When did she even leave? Last thing I remember was watching Elf and then the next thing I know, Coop was yelling and waking us up." Kai breaks the heavy silence in the room, unable to hold himself back any longer.

"Does it matter?" I ask tiredly, in the grand scheme of things, I'm not sure the time that she left last night is the biggest concern.

He jumps out of the chair, returning to pacing the length of the room, hands clenched into fists at his side.

"Yes! No, I don't know." All the energy is zapped out of him, it seems; he leans against the wall opposite us. "I just don't get why she keeps running away from us. She should've just stayed or woken one of us up to take her home." He stares at the ceiling tiles before going on high alert again, straightening to look at all of us. "Please tell me she didn't walk home in the middle of the night?"

"She took an Uber around 2 in the morning." Maverick chimes in before we can all worry about Kai's question, pinching the bridge of his nose and looking more tired by the minute.

I watch the tension melt away from Kai, and I feel it too, having some relief knowing that she wasn't wandering around Riverside alone at night.

Silence settles around us once again, each of us exhausted and lost in our own thoughts.

I can't take the waiting anymore. I need to know something. There's no reason it should take this long for an update, and it only amplifies my nerves every time I think about the clock ticking away, another hour spent not knowing.

Maverick said she was in bad shape when they brought her in.

I need to know if she's okay, if she's scared, or confused.

Just as I'm about to get up to head to the nurse's station to ask someone for any information, Eli's voice stops me in my tracks.

"Wait." His gaze zeros in on Maverick, eyes narrowed. "You knew she was leaving in the middle of the night in a car with some stranger, and you what, just let her?" His voice is icy, tinged with restrained anger just beneath the surface.

Kai stiffens; all his focus is on Maverick.

"What would you have liked me to do? She's a grown woman; I wasn't going to drag her back into the house and hold her hostage." Maverick shoots back at him, his irritation clear.

"Really? I thought you said she was nothing but a child?" Eli mocks him bitterly, throwing his words back in his face from just a few weeks ago.

I won't lie; I was thinking the same thing. I'm not stupid enough to bring that up right now, though. I can already feel the tension between us ramping up, and with it an impending migraine. Not the time that I want to deal with all of us bickering over the same crap.

Kai ignores Eli's low blow, stepping towards Maverick and matching his stance, arms crossed over his chest.

"You could have done something if you knew she was sneaking out. Did you even suggest that she stay for the night? Or wake one of us up?" He waits for an answer, but based on Maverick's cold stare, he won't be getting one. "Jesus! You had no issues holding her hostage when you brought her home when she was sick, but now suddenly you have an issue with it?"

"She can make her own decisions!" Maverick explodes, "You all treat her like she's made of glass, but that does not mean that you get to dictate where she goes and what she does. Do you ever stop to think that she's so quick to run away because all you do is smother her?"

"Since when do you give a shit?" Kai yells back, "Just last week you were insisting to us that you wanted nothing to do with her!"

I'm about to step in, ending their argument before it gets out of hand. But Maverick's demeanor shifts instantly.

He sinks back into his chair, running a hand over his tired face.

"Can we not do this right now?" He pleads.

"Now seems like as good a time as any," Kai shrugs. "All we have is time; we have no clue when Lottie will wake up."

Tension lingers between them as they stare one another down. Kai must see the underlying worry in Mav's stare because he relents, dropping back down into his seat.

“Fine, but if you’ve changed your mind and are suddenly in this with Lottie, a little heads up would be nice.”

Before Maverick can respond, a tall, older doctor strides into the room, studying papers on a clipboard. His glasses are perched so far on his nose that I’m stuck wondering how they stay on his face, and when he looks up to address us, his head levels at an odd angle to see above the frames.

“Gentlemen, I was told you all are here for Charlotte Woods?” He asks, looking between the four of us.

We all rush to stand, instantly energized after a morning of waiting. I’d feel bad for how we crowd the poor man’s personal space, but I’m too anxious to get to Charlotte.

“Is she awake? Can we see her?” Kai is the first to reach him and ask what we’re all begging to know.

Folding the clipboard under his arm, the man gestures for us to follow him. Leading us down the hall and into an elevator.

“Miss Woods' injuries were overall very mild; she is still asleep from a mild sedative we had to administer to her for her comfort.” His words carry no inflection as he continues to lead us to her room. “She has a mild concussion that we need to monitor, at least overnight, but possibly a couple of days, depending. Her clavicle is broken; she’s in a sling and will be for a few weeks. It shouldn’t cause her much discomfort; it will mostly be an inconvenience as she’ll have limited movement. Her wrist has a minor sprain as well, which will have to stay wrapped for at least a week."

We all shuffle into the room, catching sight of her for the first time since last night. She lies in a hospital bed, pale and battered. Her face is marred with dark bruises, and the sling covering her torso keeps her arm immobile. Her hair is the wildest I've ever seen it, matted and tangled in different spots, laid out across the pillow. IV lines and wires cover her, making everything look much worse than it sounds.

I barely hear the doctor as he finishes the laundry list of injuries, too engrossed in cataloging every detail I can see.

"We were told there was broken glass, which resulted in quite a few small abrasions that we cleaned, and some stitches in the back of her skull, but those should heal fine on their own." He turns to face us now that we're all situated in spots around the room. "Overall, she's fortunate not to have worse injuries. As I said, we'll monitor her, and as long as there are no complications, she will be released in a couple of days. No screens for at least a week, but she'll probably be tired, so it shouldn't be too hard to rest. The arm needs to stay immobilized until the clavicle is healed."

The doctor leaves us shortly after, when none of us have any questions for him.

Silence descends upon us, the only sound in the room coming from the heart monitor attached to Charlotte's chest.

"Who did this?" Eli rasps out, breaking the heavy silence.

"No one was there by the time I got inside," Mav's voice is choked again, forcing the words out. "I had to kick the door down, and I could hear everything inside, but when I got in, she was just lying on the floor."

None of this makes sense. We've known Charlotte for a couple of months, and she doesn't strike me as the kind of person who would have enemies out to get her.

"Lottie locked her door?" Kai asks.

"Yeah, why?"

Kai and Eli share a look but offer nothing more.

"We will come up with a way to find out who it was and why they came after her. First, we'll need to get her home and settled so she can heal." Maverick is back in his leader role, ready to make a plan and get things done. I'm not surprised; I knew his withdrawn presence from downstairs wouldn't last long.

"By home, I really hope you mean our home?" Eli asks, shooting daggers towards Maverick.

His eyes narrow at the accusing tinge to his words.

"Obviously, I'm not sending her back to her trashed dorm room where she was just attacked." Eli rolls his eyes, not appeased. "Later, I need you and Kai to go grab whatever is salvageable, see if you can clean up any of the aftermath that's left. We'll contact the school to get the rest taken care of."

"If you think I'm leaving her side, then you've clearly lost your mind."

"Yeah, we almost lost her. You can't expect us to leave her here with you." Kai is quick to agree. "No offense, but just yesterday you acted like you couldn't stand to be around her."

Maverick's jaw clenches, the vein in his forehead throbbing, a sure sign that he's about to lose his cool.

"We all just need to calm down," I decide to intervene, "Regardless of how things have gone, Mav was there for Charlotte last night." I address the twins. "I'm sure he's just as shaken up with the situation. Ease up a little." Looking to Maverick, I add, "And we're all stressed out, we don't need a drill sergeant barking orders. Right now, we're here for Charlotte and whatever she needs; the rest we can figure out later."

No one argues, thankfully, opting instead to sit and stew in their own thoughts.

The same silence that lingered in the waiting room seems to have followed us here, now interrupted by the heart monitor's beep, letting us know that Charlotte is still here.

I cling to the sound, waiting with bated breath through the silence that follows each one, needing reassurance.

I already knew that Charlotte was special, that she was someone who would come in and change us, hopefully for the better. Seeing Mav's newfound interest in her, along with my brothers', only cements the fact that she's becoming the most essential part of our lives.

None of us is willing to sit by and let anything happen to her again.

I almost feel sorry for her. If she felt smothered with our attention before, she's not going to know what to do with the attention she's about to receive now that we've all realized that the four of us are all in.

I hope it doesn't freak her out too much, because even if she tried to run, she wouldn't get far.

No one in this room would let her slip away.

2

~ Charlotte ~

Beep… Beep… Beep

Images of broken glasses and faceless men flash through my mind.

Beep… Beep… Beep

Hands wrapped around my neck, stealing any air trying to seep into my lungs.

Beep… Beep… Beep

An annoying beeping sound that won't go away.

Why is my alarm going off? And why can I not turn it off?

I must have gotten wrapped up in my weighted blanket again; my arm feels trapped against my stomach.

More images of splintered wood and debris littered the hardwood.

The faceless man, once again, was hovering over me. And… Maverick? Why is he here? Did he get rid of the man? Can he turn off my alarm? The sound is really annoying.

His lips move, but no sound comes out.

Have I gone deaf?

Wait – no. I can still hear the beeping.

Not deaf.

So why can't I hear his words?

He looks worried. I wonder why. He usually looks like an asshole, mad at the world.

Something had to have happened to put the worry lines between his brows.

I want to smooth it out, make him feel better. He's a lot cuter when he looks pissed off.

He starts to panic. I still don't know why.

It's making me worry, my heart is starting to beat faster with his panicked breathing, and I can see his chest heaving.

I can't breathe.

Are the hands back around my throat?

The beeping is louder now, much more annoying than before.

Beep. Beep. Beep. Beep. Beep. Beep.

"Charlotte! You need to calm down!"

Oh, good. I can hear again.

Maverick sounds worried. I still don't know why.

I'm just tired.

I hope he turns off my alarm soon. I just need to sleep a little longer.

Maybe when I wake up, he'll be back to normal, ignoring me and being angry at the world.

I don't know why he doesn't like me.

Maybe I can ask him when I wake up...

3

~ Maverick ~

The heart rate monitor startles me out of sleep; I don't even remember closing my eyes.

Kai and Eli are slouched over on the couch, heads thrown back as they sleep. Cooper seems to have left sometime during the night. I vaguely remember him saying he was going to grab a few things from the house.

The insistent beeping of the machine draws my attention back to Charlotte, looking pained and struggling in her bed.

Moving to her side, I try to rouse her from her nightmare, but I have no luck as she struggles away from my touch.

The monitor only increases with her panicked breaths as she fights off the demons in her mind. She fights against the sling that pins her arm in place.

I don't know what to do. I don't want her to hurt herself. I know if I can't get her to calm down, then I'll have to call a nurse, and that's only going to end with more sedatives for her, only dragging out the time before we can see her eyes on us again.

"Charlotte, you need to calm down." I lean forward to whisper in her ear, not wanting to wake the twins. "I know you're scared, and you don't know what's going on, but I'm here. I won't leave you, you're safe."

She seems to relax slightly at the sound of my voice in her ear, giving me enough room to reach up and stroke her hair. My fingers get stuck in the knots, but I gently work my way through, continuing to murmur reassurances in her ear.

What feels like an hour passes before the monitor slows down to a normal rhythm, her struggles ceasing.

Her features soften, settling into a deep, hopefully peaceful sleep.

I settle back into my seat for another long and restless night, ready to jump in and comfort her at any sign of discomfort.

The silence in the room weighs heavily on me, the only sounds being the heart monitor and the twins' quiet snores.

I know they're upset with me, and they don't understand where my emotions are at right now. Truthfully, I don't fully understand them myself. I'm exhausted and emotionally wrung out from the last 48 hours.

I do know that I meant what I told Charlotte in her room, every last word. I was stupid to try to fight the feelings that I've had for her since the day she showed up at GLS, timid but ready to stand up to me for the sake of helping her friend.

I was able to admit my feelings to her in the quiet of her dorm when I knew she couldn't hear me, but the thought of admitting it to myself, or to the guys, out loud is daunting.

Since our parents died, I've had to take on the role of the leader, putting everyone else's wants and feelings first. I've been afraid to let myself feel too deeply since they've been gone, in fear that something will come along to snatch away anything that can make me feel good.

I don't regret putting my brothers first, but seeing Charlotte lying on the floor, broken and bleeding, was a slap to the face of reality. Anything can happen at any time, and the only thing I lose by hiding my feelings is the chance to be happy. It made me realize I'm not willing to pass up that chance, as I have in the past.

The guilt from how I treated her the past few weeks, shutting her out when she's only been honest and authentic with all of us, keeps crashing into me. The only thing I can do is push it down and push forward, promising myself and her that I'll find a way to make it up to her.

The night is long and restless, Charlotte stirring every hour, fighting the demons in her mind. But there isn't anywhere else I'd rather be than right here by her side, paying my penance.

***

Voices filling the room rouse me from sleep. My neck aches from the awkward angle of lying on the side of the bed, stretched out from my chair at Charlotte's bedside.

Pulling myself up off the chair, I take a moment to stretch out my neck before taking in the rest of the room.

A new doctor stands by the door, looking uncomfortable as she watches Kai pace the length of the room. Eli stands with arms crossed against the far wall, shooting daggers her way while Cooper is off to the other side of the bed, looking as confused as I feel.

"What's happening?" I ask, glancing over Charlotte to make sure she's still peacefully asleep. She remains unbothered in her bed, thankfully looking relaxed for once.

"Lottie's been drugged!" Kai explodes, spinning around to continue pacing.

"What?"

Cooper sighs, "She wasn't drugged." He argues, met with a disgruntled sound from Eli.

Still at a loss, I look to the doctor for some clarity.

"I was going over charts this morning with the shift change and just had some questions about Ms. Wood's medications. I was trying to get some clarity on that."

"What's wrong with her medications?" I vaguely remember Charlotte telling me that she took something for her anxiety, but I'd never asked for more details beyond that.

"The fact that her parents have her taking shit that she doesn't need!" Kai chimes in, looking angrier by the second.

This is getting me nowhere but more confused.

"Why wouldn't she need it? I thought it was just anxiety meds?"

"Her parents have her taking Ritalin," Eli offers, when it's clear that I don't know what that means. He continues. "It's a medication usually used for people with ADHD, not Asperger's."

"That's actually not a correct diagnosis anymore; we no longer use the term Asperger's." The doctor chimes in. "We tend to use ASD – autism spectrum disorder, which I also would want to talk to Ms. Woods when she's awake to assess further to see if that's even the correct diagnosis for her. It's been so long since she's seen a doctor, and medical knowledge has come a long way even in the last couple of years."

That's so much information to process at once, and I'm still not seeing where Kai's anger is coming from and if it's just a result of his exhaustion and stress.

"So, the medication she's been taking, it's just not useful to her?"

The doctor tilts her head from side to side, considering.

"Most likely, people with autism tend to react differently to Ritalin than individuals with ADHD. In some cases, it can cause an *increase* in anxiety and sensory overload when prescribed incorrectly. So, I obviously would like her to stop taking it, and when she's awake and feeling more alert, I want to set up an appointment with her to discuss further."

I'm too stunned to speak, and after a couple of vitals checks, she leaves us to the silence of the room again.

"I can't believe this shit." Eli spits, dropping down onto the couch, pulling his glasses off, and dragging a hand down his face.

"Fuck her parents, this is seriously screwed up." Kai agrees, dropping down beside him.

Coop and I share a look of confusion, "We don't know her parents knew any better; it could have been an honest mistake." His words sound weak; we've all heard bits and pieces of her home life with her parents, and it's anything but a happy and nurturing environment.

"Her parents forced her to take the meds even after she went to college in return for funding her tuition." Kai spits, "They've had her drugged since she started high school because they think she's not normal or some shit."

The silence falls around us once again while we all contemplate the fucked-up reality of Charlotte's family situation. And again, the guilt of how I treated her rears its ugly head, washing over me and drowning me back in a pit of depression.

“Right now, we just need to focus on getting Charlotte healed; the rest we can deal with later."

We all grunt our agreement with Coop and settle in for hours of discomfort, hoping Charlotte will come around at some point.

I try to use the time to stay on top of some work emails so that everything runs smoothly when we get back to work, but my mind keeps drifting to how to make it up to Charlotte once she’s awake and back home.

I’m new to showing emotions, and that’s going to be enough of a struggle. But it seems I also have to get used to groveling in my future as well.

4

~ Charlotte ~

The beeping is back.

I hate that sound. At least this time, I don't have the random faceless man trying to kill me.

And this time, I can hear voices? Muffled voices fluttering around me like dandelions in the wind.

I latch onto one of the voices; it sounds like Kai. My sweet, sweet Kai. I wonder what he's doing here.

With a flash of light, my sight changes, dropping me somewhere else completely. Looking around, I see I'm on the river walk, sun shining, breeze blowing, and sailboats gliding across the St. John's.

Suddenly, I see him, Kai, walking along the riverwalk, pointing out manatee shadows in the water. It's like watching a movie play out before me, but I see myself walking hand in hand with Kai. The sun shines brightly on both of us, reflecting off my hair and casting glimmering sparks in his eyes as he stares at me, laughing as if I've never been happier.

I can remember that at that moment, I was happier than I had been in a long time.

This was our first date – the first time he took me out, just the two of us.

I lose sight of us for a moment, spinning around to see where we went, only to see us standing at the water's edge in the park a few blocks from where I was moments ago.

I watch myself as I toss pieces of bread towards the waiting flock of ducks flapping around in the water, giggling like a little schoolgirl. I study Kai as his attention is fixed on my face, studying my expression with a soft smile of admiration on his face. He doesn't glance at the animals before us, staring at my face like he's trying to commit it to memory.

I can't do anything but watch, mesmerized at the affection and care that shines from him as he stands beside me. Watching closely as he catches every little detail. He hands me pieces of bread each time I run out before I even have to ask. His hand carefully grabs the back of my jacket when I lean a little too close to the wall separating us from the water to get a closer look at the ducks. His eyes sparkle and match my amusement with every laugh or observation spoken aloud, his hidden dimple appearing on his cheek as he laughs with me.

All the silent observations fill me with warmth, like I can feel the sun shining on my skin even now, trapped in a memory.

I try to step closer, to get a better look at him and maybe catch a few of the words we shared. But every time I step forward, I see the two of us shift further and further away, making it impossible to reach them. Each time I try to step closer, and they shift away, they become harder to see, blurring into two faceless strangers, and the world around me begins to dissipate like smoke, and flickers of Eli's voice sound around me.

As the smoke clears, I find myself in a new place. I can smell the crisp smell of freshly brewed coffee. Looking around, I see the coffee shop in Riverside, just down the street from GLS, Urban Bean. Empty mugs litter the tables, faceless strangers occupy some of the seats, and a gentle hum of conversation fills the space.

Looking at the corner booth by the front windows, I find us.

I sit on one side of the booth, hands wrapped around a large mug, blowing lightly on my steaming drink, looking shyly at Eli across from me. He looks much more relaxed, but a closer look shows subtle signs. His hand, not holding his cup of coffee, is fisted in his lap, balancing on his bouncing leg under the table. Each time I'm not looking across the table at him, I see him fidget with his glasses or run his hand through his hair – his nervous tic.

Something I say to him makes him bark out a laugh, and I strain to catch a piece of our conversation, to just remember what was said.

"I've never heard of someone's favorite animal being a turtle." He snorts, then, seeing my quickly reddening cheeks, he adds, "Why a turtle?"

I watch as I fight through my embarrassment, determined to stick to our game of twenty questions and not avoid the topic.

"You didn't let me finish," I try to playfully roll my eyes, but it comes across as forced and awkward. "My favorite is a sea turtle." I clarify, "And I like them because they always look so tranquil and peaceful, content in their shells. In my mind, they don't see a need to change for anyone; they are as they are, and that's enough for them."

Eli's face transforms at my explanation, shifting from teasing to understanding. His leg ceases bouncing, and a small smile pulls at his lips, quickly disappearing behind his mug while he tags a drag of his coffee, and I mimic him, enjoying the silence.

"Well, that beats my answer of dragons because they breathe fire." He jokes.

"That and there's no proof that dragons were even real," I add.

His face becomes serious, "Don't get me started on this debate. I'm well too prepared for this and will win."

That tears a laugh from me, but before I hear anymore of our conversation, I see the scene before me disappearing again.

I catch Cooper and Maverick's voices, seeing quick flashes of the day they took me to the rage room, before I find myself in a hockey rink with a rowdy cheering crowd and Cooper by my side.

A child-like amusement lights up his face as he grins at the fight breaking out on the ice, shoveling handfuls of popcorn into his mouth.

"You seem to really be into the violence," I observe, stealing a piece of popcorn for myself while watching him.

"Oh, this is nothing, you should see some of the fights that used to break out back in the day, back when my dad would take Mav and me to the amateur games when we were kids." His excitement ramps up even further as he reminisces.

I watch my smile widen, clearly imagining a young Cooper and Maverick, over the moon at getting to watch something so exciting with their dad.

"He would take just the two of you?"

All of his attention is directed to me as the fight comes to an end and the teams are sent back to their respective benches.

"Yeah, we were really young when he started taking us for 'father and sons bonding time,' and then the twins came along, and my mom thought they were too young to go. It kind of just stuck as being our thing after that."

We sit in a comfortable silence for a few minutes, snacking on popcorn and watching until the end of the second period, before I ask another question.

"Have you and Maverick been to any games since he died?" I ask him gently.

He's lost in thought for a moment, looking over the crowd of people below us.

"No, Mav has refused to go ever since. But I've missed this." A somber smile pulls at his lips while he looks at me, reaching over to take my hand in his. "I figure this could be our thing now, if you want?"

I watch my eyes become misty, honored that he wants to share what is obviously a sacred time with me.

I already know my feelings for him and his brothers run deep, but watching it play out before me only cements the fact that I'm in way deeper than I ever imagined I could be.

All too soon, the scene disappears, leaving me in a cloud of smoke and lost in the depths of darkness. I catch bits and pieces of the guy's voices around me, but I'm not able to latch onto them enough to make sense of what's being said.

I'm left alone and confused, wondering where I am and how I can get back to them.

And that damn beeping is back.

5

~ Kai ~

It's been two days.

Christmas came and went. What was supposed to be an awesome day, full of family and fun, was spent in a fucking hospital room with all of us waiting and hoping for Lottie to just open her eyes and tell us she's okay.

My nerves are shot, and I've run through every emotion possible sitting here in this room.

I was so heated yesterday at the thought of Lottie's parents drugging her with prescription pills for years, possibly knowing that they were doing more harm than good in the hopes of making her 'normal'. Cooper had dragged me out of the hospital to help him while he went to Lottie's dorm and collected some of her things to take home. That had only made my mood even more sour.

Seeing the state of her room and all of the destruction made my blood boil. Cooper kept me at the house to shower and eat, waiting until I had calmed down before he would let me go back to be by her side.

We've all been reluctant to leave her side. Mav and Eli have left only once or twice to shower, eat, or handle work matters.

Cooper seems to have temporarily taken on the role of leader among us, with Mav too lost in his own thoughts to boss us around as he typically would. Finding Lottie must have really shaken him up more than any of us thought; he's barely spoken since we met him at the hospital the other night.

I know the doctors are doing what they need to do, which is let Lottie rest, but I'd be lying if I said resentment wasn't building up inside me with each passing hour that she doesn't wake.

They say her body is just trying to heal, and that her mind is just protecting itself. If they would just wake her up, then I can protect her.

I settle into the rock-hard sofa, ready for another restless night of waiting, just listening to the soft beeping of the heart rate monitor in the corner.

The door opening pulls me from another fitful sleep, and morning light filtering through the blinds lets me know it's morning again. Shifting around to get comfortable to try and catch a few more hours of rest, I expect to hear one of the nurses shuffle around to check on Lottie.

"What in God's name is going on here?" The deep and unfamiliar voice startles me, instantly shunning the remnants of sleep and putting me on alert.

Looking to the door, I'm met with two unfamiliar faces. An older man, tall with dark hair and frown lines etched into his aged face, and a woman who bears a startling resemblance to Lottie, about thirty years older, look around the room, taking in the four of us in various stages of sleep.

"Mr. and Mrs.Woods," Cooper stands to greet Lottie's parents, offering a hand to both of them, which they both look at before continuing to look around the small, yet crowded room. "I'm Cooper Locke, one of Charlotte's bosses. It's nice to meet you." He finally pulls his hand back, tucking it into his pocket awkwardly.

"Boss? Since when does Charlotte have a job?" Her father all but barks out, while Coop and I exchange a confused look.

"For months now," I chime in. "She started working with us halfway through last semester."

Their attention sways to me, giving me a once-over that doesn't try to hide their dissatisfaction.

"And you are?" Her mother asks.

"Kai." I don't offer anything more, not that they seem to mind. It's clear that Lottie hasn't shared much of her personal life with them, not that I blame her after a minute of knowing them.

"And the other two?" Her father eyes Mav and Eli, where they sit across the room, now awake and watching the strange interaction.

“Maverick Locke,” Mav sits with folded arms, not offering any pleasantries.

Eli stands to offer a hand, much like Coop.

“Eli,” He too pulls his hand away awkwardly when they both do nothing more than stare at it like an alien life form before them.

“So the four of you work with Charlotte, why are you all piled into her room sleeping like a bunch of homeless men?” Her father asks, stepping closer to her bedside to take an uninterested glance over the damage written all over her body.

“Because we care about her, and we didn’t want her to be alone.” Eli offers.

Her father snorts, as if the thought of it is laughable.

“Well, consider yourselves excused,” He adjusts his cufflinks, not sparing any of us a second glance. “We’ll have Charlotte transferred to our local hospital so that we can take her home once she’s cleared.”

Mav springs up from the couch, immediately on the defensive.

“Home? You can’t just take her home.”

Looking directly at Mav for the first time, Lottie’s mother blinks.

“And why would we not be able to take our daughter home?”

My annoyance flares at her lack of common sense and her focus on her own daughter's personal life or happiness.

"Because she has a life here! She has a job, and she's graduating in just a few months; you can't just take her away from that." I butt in before Mav can say anything. Judging from the fury flaring in his eyes, his response was going to be anything but cordial.

"And look where that got her, lying in a hospital bed, black and blue." Her mother spits, "We knew letting her live on her own was a mistake; clearly, it's too much for her, and she can't handle it."

What the fuck was this woman's problem?

"Are you insinuating that Lottie getting attacked was *her* fault?"

"*Charlotte* is not like you; she's different. She can't handle everyday things the same way that you would. This is an example of what happens when we let her attempt things that she can't handle." Her mother explains all of this with little interest and no inflection in her tone, as if she's reading the weather report for the day.

"Is that why you've had her drugged with prescription pills for years now?" Cooper jumps in, his temper obviously flaring now, his calm and friendly demeanor gone.

You could hear a pin drop with the silence that overtakes the room.

Tension thickens in the air as we wait for their response.

"*Drugged*," Her father snorts, "Her *medication* helps her in ways that you couldn't possibly understand. And quite frankly, I don't see how that is any of your concern as her boss."

"I don't know what back-alley therapist you had prescribe her that shit, but it most definitely doesn't *help* her." Mav snorts, matching his energy. "Maybe you'd be interested to hear what her doctor had to say, mainly that her medication, which you force her to take, actually worsens her anxiety and sensory overload."

"So basically, it's you who has made her symptoms worse and made her *different* than the rest of us," I add salt to the wound.

It's clear that the only thing they care about is appearances, and any inkling of Lottie being different or unique from other people is a flaw in their eyes.

Her mother gasps, metaphorically clutching her pearls.

"You don't know anything! We only ever did what was best for her."

"Best for her or best for you?" I ask what we're all thinking.

"Best for all of us!" Her mother all but yells, "You don't know what it's like to have a daughter like her. One that's so difficult, and that all the other parents whisper about behind your back. We just wanted her to be normal!"

My heart cracks in my chest, catching a glimpse of the parents that Lottie has had to deal with her entire life.

Parents who are so vastly different from the ones I was blessed with. My parents loved us for who we were; hell, they'd even handpicked Eli and me to be a part of their family with Mav and Coop. They would never try to change us or mold us to be anything but who we are. And to hear Lottie's parents stand here and blatantly say that they couldn't stand who she is makes my heart ache for her.

An audible gasp sounds out behind us. Swinging around, I'm instantly met with those gorgeous green eyes I've been missing the last two days. Currently, filled with fear and confusion as Lottie takes in the scene before her, and the unshed tears I can see her holding back tell me she heard her mother's confession.

Mav goes to say something else, oblivious to Lottie waking up. Their conversation continues, but ignoring everyone in the room, I take the few steps to her bedside.

She tears her gaze away from the others and focuses on me as I sink onto the bed next to her, grabbing her free hand in mine.

"Hey, Lottie-girl. How are you feeling?"

She doesn't answer me, squeezing my hand in a death grip while her eyes trail over her arm in the sling and our surroundings, lingering on her parents before looking back to me with furrowed brows.

"Everything's going to be okay," I promise her. Leaning forward, I brush a kiss on her temple, careful not to touch her anywhere that she's cut or bruised.

"Hey, she's awake." I hear Coop interrupt the conversation behind us, probably hoping to prevent them from saying anything else that could upset her.

"Thank God!" Her mother strides over to the other side of the bed, looking down at her daughter. "Charlotte, we are getting you away from these people and taking you home *today*."

I didn't think she could grip my hand any harder, but the knuckles in my hand crack as she tightens her death grip even further. Shaking her head vehemently at her mother's suggestion.

"Not this mute crap again. Charlotte, use your words!" Her mother's face becomes a mask of disgust.

"Mute?" I can't help but ask.

"Whenever Charlotte wants to avoid doing something, she turns to not speaking. *Selective mutism*. It's a petulant way of avoiding responsibilities."

"Who can blame her? I'm ready to become mute after talking to you for five minutes." Mav mutters loud enough for us to hear.

Eli and I choke back our laughs while her parents shoot daggers at Mav.

Throwing his hands to the side, he steps up to the side of her bed, hovering over her to put a fist on either side of her hips so he can look her in the eyes, drawing her attention to him.

"Charlotte, do you want to go home with your parents?" He asks.

No hesitation, she shakes her head back and forth.

"Do you want your parents here?"

Again, she shakes her head, clearly showing her answer.

"Do you feel comfortable coming to stay with us while your dorm gets repaired and while you heal?"

I bristle at the thought of her ever going to stay in her dorm alone again, but a subtle headshake from Coop keeps me in check as we watch Lottie contemplate for a moment before nodding her head softly at the offer.

"And do you want to finish out school and graduate in a couple of months and keep working at GLS?"

Another nod.

With a curt nod of his own, he turns to look at both her parents, a smug expression now sitting on his face after having proven his point.

"Seems pretty clear to me," He shrugs, "She wants to stay here and fulfill her responsibilities."

Her mother goes to say something, but her father quickly cuts her off.

"You think you know what you're getting into, then fine, she's your problem then." Grabbing her mother by the wrist, he makes his way out of the room, "I told you driving down here was a waste of time."

The door shuts behind them, excusing them as swiftly as they'd appeared and with no parting words for their only daughter, who still has a death grip on my hand.

"Don't listen to them, Lottie. I know they're your parents, but they honestly suck." Squeezing her hand, I try to loosen her grip so I can feel my fingers again.

Mav shakes his head, "Understatement of the year."

"How are you feeling, Charlie?" Eli asks, drawing our attention back to her.

She refrains from speaking, only shrugging her shoulders in response. We all exchange semi-worried glances, wondering why she's not speaking. I know her parents said she's done this before, but I wouldn't trust them as far as I could throw their overdressed asses.

"Do you remember what happened?" Coop asks, leaning around Mav to get a closer look at her.

She waits a moment, chewing on her bottom lip before nodding softly.

Before we can ask anything else, a huge yawn tears free from her, and her eyes droop, showing her exhaustion. I can feel her hand slipping from mine as she quickly falls closer to sleep.

"Rest for a little while, and we can talk later," I suggest, squeezing her hand and kissing her forehead once more, watching her eyes fall shut as I pull away.

We sit silently for a few minutes, making sure that she's fully asleep before talking.

"What the fuck was that shit?" I hiss, trying to keep my voice down.

"I've never met parents who are so disconnected from their child. They had no remorse for practically drugging her for years when you brought up what the doctor said!" Eli fumes.

"Unfortunately, not everyone is blessed with good parents as we had." Coop reminds us. All of us fall silent again at the mention of our parents, lost in our own thoughts.

Coop moves to leave the room, "I'm going to let the doctor know that she woke up and maybe mention that she's not talking."

Mav and I still sit on opposite sides of her bed, sandwiching her between us. Eli eyes him skeptically, taking his spot back on the couch.

"You were quick to step up to her parents and defend her." He observes.

"Your point?" Mav asks with a dry look.

"Nothing, it's just becoming very evident that you care."

Mav doesn't respond as he pulls himself off the bed, stretching and grabbing a water from the small fridge on the counter before dropping beside Eli on the small couch.

"You told me to decide what I wanted, and I did. Don't tell me now you have a problem seeing me put her first?"

Stretching back, Eli gets comfortable, dropping his head to the back of the couch and closing his eyes.

“No, no problem. Just glad to see you pull your head out of your ass after all.”

“Let’s see if he keeps it there, that’s the real test.” I laugh.

Mav shoots daggers at both of us, but refrains from responding; he knows that we’re due to give him a hard time after how much he refused Lottie. He never stood a chance; it was always a losing game.

6

~ Maverick ~

Four days.

Four days within these stark white walls, with the strong smell of antiseptic filling my senses and the depressing sounds of people's misfortunes filtering through the walls.

Finally, today we get to leave, with Charlotte cleared to go home by the doctors. She still hasn't spoken since she woke up, but the doctor from the second day that we were here kicked us out of the room to have a chance to explain more in depth what she told us about her medication and the possibility of getting an updated diagnosis.

Of all the staff that had been in and out over the days, she was my favorite. She kept us all in the loop and gave us clear, concise options for what could best help Charlotte.

She told us that selective mutism is common for people with ASD, and could be worsened by the recent trauma that she's gone through. Our job was to help Charlotte with her recovery and offer her support, so she feels comfortable enough to start talking again. We also were supposed to watch for any signs of a spike in anxiety or her sensory overload so that we could know what she needs the most help with – if any.

We only know that her parents had her on a medication that worsened her comorbidities; we don't actually know how she'll be without the meds. After meeting her parents, I imagine whatever she struggles with off the meds is nothing like what they made it out to be. I think they were more the problem than anything.

I sent the other three to go grab breakfast and bring the car around so that she would have a couple of minutes alone to get dressed without being hovered over like a wounded animal. She might not be using her words right now, but her face reads like a book, and this morning, it was full of overwhelmed anxiety as she tried to just catch her breath once the doctor said she could leave.

I knew I was the best option to stay with her, because as far as she was concerned, I still didn't like her. And at the moment, that worked in my favor; it meant there were no expectations on her end for me being anything other than a jackass.

So, I got to stay and watch over her, and my brothers got to run all the errands.

Currently, I was watching her stubbornly try to put on her shoes without asking for any help. One arm in a sling and barely able to bend over, and she still didn't want to ask.

She'd managed to get dressed in the loose sweats and t-shirt that Coop had brought her, only because the nurse followed her into the bathroom to 'help' without giving her any choice.

Another twenty minutes of standing by while she brushed her teeth and combed her hair without so much as a glance in my direction.

This was the most entertainment I've had in days.

The little furrow between her brows as she concentrated fully on every task was borderline adorable. But I was mostly just relieved to see her acting like her usual overly stubborn self.

I let her struggle for another minute or two before she finally huffs out a breath and drops the shoe to the floor, sucking in a deep breath before flicking a glance in my direction.

Her reluctant, silent admission of needing help.

Normally, I would hold her to her little staring match, waiting until she folded before making her ask for what she needed. That's obviously not an option here, and she seems frustrated enough, either because she knows she needs help or because she can't find her words right now. Either way, I'll cave this time.

Grabbing the shoe, I kneel down, reaching out to catch her foot. She jumps slightly at the contact, raising a brow. I wait until she relaxes before slipping the shoe on and tying the laces, then move to the other.

"You ready to go?"

She just looks from her newly tied shoes to me.

"I'll take that as a yes."

I step out into the hall to grab the wheelchair that was left for her, enjoying the hard stare she gives me as I enter the room with it.

Stopping at her bedside, I gesture for her to get in, and she gives me a firm headshake.

"Sorry, hospital policy," I tell her unapologetically.

She scowls the entire time I help lift her off the side of the bed and steady her before guiding her into the cushioned seat of the chair.

"Don't worry, I'm sure you'll only need help for a little while, then you'll be back to your stubborn ways of making everything harder by insisting on doing it yourself." I barely miss her good hand as she reaches over her head to slap at me, making me fight to conceal my laugh.

She won't be like this for long, though, so I'm going to poke fun where I can about her having to actually let us help.

The others are out front and waiting by the time we make it downstairs, standing by the car with flowers, an energy drink, and breakfast in hand.

Kiss-asses.

I just manage not to shove Kai out of the way when he moves to lift her into the back seat, opting to return the wheelchair before jumping into the driver's seat.

Both the twins have her sandwiched between them in the back seat, working together to pull her seatbelt over her without disturbing the sling over her chest. Cooper slumps in the passenger seat, the exhaustion from the last couple of days showing clearly in the bags under his eyes. While the twins and I have practically been glued to her side, he's taken point of making sure her room was all set up for her at the house so she wasn't coming home with us to an empty and unfamiliar space.

He told me about her room briefly this morning, but I've yet to see it. I'm sure it will be perfect, seeing how he decorated her office at GLS. I trust his judgement, and it wasn't like I've been very useful since I brought her here, lost in my own head.

Once we get her home, I'm hoping I can get myself back on track with work and maybe lose some of the tension that's been coiled up in me since I answered my phone on Christmas.

The drive is relatively quiet; the twins speak softly to Charlotte in the back seat about nothing, just trying to break the never-ending silence looming over us.

I turn on the radio and set it to play a Taylor Swift playlist. The twins go quiet at my choice, and Cooper shoots me an odd look, but thankfully, none of them comment. I know it was the right choice when I watch Charlotte's shoulders relax through the rearview mirror.

The same exhaustion I see weighing on Cooper hits me the moment that I park in the driveway, the weight of the last week finally landing on my shoulders, and my walls slightly crumbling now that I'm back in my safe space.

I head into the house, unlock the door, and make sure Zeus is calm while the twins help Charlotte out of the car.

She obviously hasn't voiced any objections to us hovering over her, but we all have seen how stubborn she can be. Sooner rather than later, she's going to crack.

I keep my gaze on Zeus running laps in the backyard and watch from the corner of my eye as the twins bring Charlotte in and get her settled on the couch. They flock around her like mother hens, grabbing her blankets, water, snacks, and that stupid weighted dinosaur Cooper bought her while she sits stiffly in the middle.

Cooper must notice her discomfort as well, leaning over the couch to tell her he's going to head upstairs and take a nap if she needs anything. There's a marginal flash of relief on her face when he says it, the realization that not all four of us will be watching her like a hawk.

The twins rush upstairs to shower and change, yelling over their shoulder at me to watch her until they're back, as if she's an infant that needs constant supervision.

It's not like she's going to slip out to go back to her dorm. She acknowledged when she woke up in the hospital that she remembers some of what happened, so she knows her dorm is trashed. Plus, I can't imagine her wanting to go back there after that.

I mentally pat myself on the back for being one of the more rational of my brothers for once.

Once the twins are gone, Charlotte melts into the couch, sighing heavily as she drops her head onto the back of the couch, closing her eyes.

The TV remote the twins handed her remains on the cushion beside her, untouched as she soaks in the silence.

I take the time to really look over her. She's battered and bruised all over, making her look even smaller than normal. Her slightly sunken cheeks and her pale complexion make her look even more frail than I've ever seen.

I let Zeus in the house, signaling for him to stay quiet in case she's already fallen asleep. He trots across the room, sniffing at her legs as his tail wags excitedly. Slowly, as if sensing that she shouldn't be bothered, he climbs up onto the couch and gently settles onto her lap.

She startles, eyes springing open at the contact, but relaxes quickly when she realizes it's him. She uses her good hand to stroke his head while his tail thumps against the cushions.

I grab myself a water, stopping at the entryway to the kitchen to catch Charlotte's attention.

Sensing my presence, her eyes meet mine.

"I'll be in my office if you need anything," I tell her. At her nod, I add a small forewarning. "The twins are going to be all over you, so if you feel smothered, come let me know. Don't run off because you feel overwhelmed." I level a stare at her, unable to help myself from calling her out about Christmas Eve.

I know it hit the mark when all she offers is an eye roll, directing her attention back to Zeus.

Heading into my office, I give her the last couple of minutes of solitude that she'll have for a while before the twins re-emerge and settle in to get some work done.

Unlike the last time she was here, I'm not shutting myself away to hide from the emotions she evokes in me. I'm determined to find any information I can about the motherfucker that broke into her room and decided to beat her half to death.

Normally, this is the type of job I would pull Eli into, hacking into any cameras we can find near her dorm and possibly even hacking into Charlotte's personal hard drive if need be. But I know my brother, and his infatuation with her means that he won't be willing to help without fessing up to her and letting her know what I'm doing.

Luckily, I have other hackers on my team who can get the job done, but it just won't be as quick since they're all on their own assignments. Regardless of how long it takes, I will find out who was behind this.

I may have just admitted my feelings for her, but I'll be dammed if anyone thinks they can rip her away from us that easily. My family has experienced enough loss to last a lifetime; we wouldn't survive losing her now that she's crashed into our lives and blended her story with ours.

I'm all in, and until she tells me to fuck off, I'll do what I can to protect her.

7

~ Charlotte ~

I'm thankful for the guys, I really am… But I've only been out of the hospital for about three hours, and they're going to drive me crazy.

Kai and Eli have piled every blanket in the house over me, which, paired with Zeus, is causing me to overheat. Anytime I shift to get cooled off or more comfortable, I have eyes on me, Zeus included!

Eli has asked me twelve different times if I want more water or a snack, and Kai keeps checking with me if there's anything else I've thought to watch.

Both of them were disappointed when they came downstairs to find me cuddling with Zeus on the couch, not leaving either of them much room to get close to me. I had to fight back my laughter at the looks on their faces when they realized I wasn't going to shoo him away so they could get closer.

It wouldn't be so bad if they would actually watch the show that they put on, or played on their phones, or did anything other than watch me from the corner of their eyes, waiting for me to need something.

I get that they were scared while I was in the hospital, when I'd finally woken up, I was a bit scared. Though that was overshadowed by my parents' arrival and what they had to tell the guys.

It wasn't a shock to me to hear the words my mother had spat out, but I noticed the guys' reactions and knew that they all felt sorry for me. It was quite a way to return to the land of the living, and a real damper on my mood, since the whole time I was asleep, I was seeing flashes of all the dates I'd had with Eli, Kai, and Cooper. So far, waking up only meant that I felt a shit ton of pain, got to hear my parents' feelings for me, and got watched like a psych patient on a seventy-two-hour hold.

The only person offering a sense of normalcy at the moment is Maverick. He's his usual guarded, distant self, and he hasn't even tried to broach the subject of my calling him to help me the other night. His lack of romantic interest in me is proving to be a benefit at the moment.

I never thought I would be referring to Maverick as 'normal,' but here we are.

Seeing the guys' memories while I was asleep made me feel loved. Seeing their expressions as they looked at me let me see their emotions and that they meant what they said about their feelings for me. Since waking up, though, they all seem so timid and afraid to touch me. It's like all the progress we've made getting closer over the last few weeks is just being trashed now that I got attacked.

On top of that, I'm sure the doctor relayed to them what she discussed with me. With my incorrect diagnosis, I'm sure they're starting to think that I'm more trouble than I'm worth with that. I've spent years with my daily alarm, swallowing tiny little pills at the request of my parents, to only find out that they don't do anything for me. Now, I'm just living in confusion, wondering what is wrong with me to make me so different than everyone else, if it's not what I've always been told.

I don't like the feeling that they're sticking with me out of pity, and that's the only thing running through my mind since waking up and seeing how they're acting, and feeling the distance they're all putting between us.

A couple more hours of awkward TV pass by uneventfully. Eli and Kai finally resort to scrolling on their phones when they get bored enough, and Cooper joins us in the living room while Maverick takes his place in the kitchen to cook dinner.

Kai and Eli hover close by as I ease myself up off the couch, my joints protesting the movement after sitting still for so long.

Sitting around the table, we end up in the same spots as we did on Christmas Eve, Maverick to my right, Cooper to my left, and the twins across from me. Of course, Zeus has his head perched on my lap, hoping for scraps.

Maverick's laid out a spread of homemade French fries, chicken tenders, salad, and an array of dipping sauces. Without asking, he grabs my plate, filling it with small portions of each, then gives it back to me and fills a ramekin with ranch, setting it by my plate as well.

Surprise flickers through me at the thoughtfulness of the gesture, but a quick glance down reminds me of the sling across my chest, making it difficult for me to fend for myself, and I'm reminded of the pity being tossed my way.

We all remain fairly quiet as we eat, lost in our own thoughts or maybe just exhausted from the last few days. Maverick doesn't even comment when he catches me giving Zeus a chicken tender, just narrows his eyes before diverting his attention.

"I think I'm going to turn in early, I'm beat, and it's been a long few days," Cooper announces once the dishes are cleared.

Nodding my head, I agree with him, not wanting to get roped into another few hours of awkward couch time, and honestly, I am ready to have some alone time and just crash.

"I'll show you to your room, if you want." He offers me, waiting at the bottom of the steps.

I look around at the other three, all watching me with varying levels of interest. I want to tell them goodnight and thank you for dinner and for everything, really. But the words are like ash in my mouth and stuck in my throat; I just can't get them to come out.

I know they'll come to me again, having felt this suffocating silence before in my life, but having your words stolen from you never gets any easier.

Kai, always realizing when I'm struggling, steps over to where I'm waiting, brushing a loose strand of hair off my face, waiting for my eyes to meet his.

"Goodnight, Lottie Girl." His lips brush my forehead. "I'm just down the hall if you need anything."

Stepping back, he leaves room for Eli to step into his place.

"Night, Charlie. I'll see you in the morning." He reaches out to squeeze my good hand before stepping back.

Maverick doesn't look up from the dishes, so I move to follow Cooper up the steps. He leads me up to the landing and to the left, on the side where his room and Maverick's sit.

Maverick's room sits at the end of the hall, with the double doors closed, blocking his space off from the outside world.

I of course, had been in there at least once, when he brought me over when I was sick, but any of the other times I've been here, the doors always remain closed. Much like him, I guess.

Cooper's room sits on the left side of the hallway, facing the front of the house, leaving another two doors on the right side of the hall.

He leads me to the door furthest from Maverick's, leaving one last door between the two.

Once the door opens, he steps aside to invite me in.

The space is a perfect blend of my office at GLS and my dorm room back at Oceancoast. The dark green weighted comforter covering the queen-sized bed in the middle of the room is almost identical to mine. The blackout curtains with star cutouts are like the ones in my office, same as the plush rugs on either side of the bed. The familiar weighted dinosaur waits at the top of the bed, and small fairy lights are strung up on the wall over the head of the bed. Over in the corner, a computer desk sits with two new monitors waiting to be used.

The walls are very plain, but I'm used to that, and the familiarity of the smaller details makes the space feel instantly welcoming.

"The bathroom is just next door; it should have everything you need, but just let us know if you're missing anything." Cooper tells me from the doorway, "I'm across the hall, and Mav is at the end."

I spin around to face him, nodding to let him know I heard him. I really want to tell him that I appreciate all the work he's clearly put into making the room perfect for me to stay here, but I'm still stuck on mute.

His eyes roam over my face before he steps into me, running a hand up my good arm to rest on my shoulder.

"I'm glad you're here with us. Just get some rest and don't hesitate to come get one of us if you need."

He retreats from the room, leaving me to myself and blissful silence. Sitting on the edge of the bed, I melt into the mattress and the way that it threatens to swallow me whole.

I was obviously asleep for a few days while in the hospital, but I would never know with how exhausted I feel. It's nice to have a private space to myself to decompress and try to organize my thoughts about all the guys and where we stand with everything that's happened. I don't want to lose them, but I don't know how they feel with all they've learned and dealt with so far.

I plan to use my new space to get my thoughts in order and to get back to work on my search for Ivy first thing tomorrow. For tonight, my only plan is to settle in under this weighted blanket and just sleep.

***

Crashing glass sounds around me as my shoulder cracks against the floor.

My glasses fly off my face as my head bounces on the hardwood, and a crushing weight settles on my chest.

Trying to fight it off, I can only make out blurred images of a faceless man wearing all black.

I'm helpless, trying to buck against their heavy weight, but with my arms pinned under their legs, I don't have much to fight with.

Knowing what comes next, I try to brace myself, but I have to suffer through as the hands wrap around my hair, slamming my head down repeatedly, until I start to feel a sticky warmth spreading across the back of my skull. Then the hands switch, wrapping around my throat, cutting off any chance I have at sucking air into my lungs.

My ears ring from the lack of oxygen, I can no longer hear myself choking, and the image hovering over me fades into nothing but darkness as I feel the hands slip away from my neck.

Even if I'm free from the hands that were pinning me down, I'm lost in a new abyss, alone and isolated, I'm free-falling into a black hole with no end in sight.

I scream out for the guys, hoping one of them can come and save me again. Unlike before, there's no savior crashing in at the last second, and there's no flashes of the guys to keep me sane.

I'm left all alone, and for the first time in my life, I don't prefer it.

***

8

~ Charlotte ~

Hands shake my shoulder, rousing me from sleep.

Instantly, I'm on alert, my heart pounding and sweat clinging to my skin. Immediately, I start fighting, not wanting to be pulled back into the darkness.

"Charlotte! Stop!" This is new; the faceless man hasn't spoken until now. And he knows my name.

Regardless, I won't let him drag me back, so I continue to fight, ignoring the stabbing pain in my arm and shoulder.

Swinging wildly, I feel my hand hit something, followed by a curse.

"Fuck, ow! Damnit, stop!" The hands latch on even harder to my good hand and my shoulder, pushing me down into the floor, and the weight settles down on my legs, stopping them from kicking, and leaving me immobile.

"Lottie! Maverick, fuck, you're crushing her!"

"I'm barely putting any weight on her!"

"What the fuck is going on? Why are you on top of her?"

All of the voices screaming out clue me in that this isn't the faceless man talking; I'm somewhere else completely.

Opening my eyes, I'm blinded by the overhead light shining behind Maverick's head, which is hovering inches over mine. A glance over his shoulder shows me Cooper, Eli, and Kai in the doorway.

What the fuck did I do now to end up in this situation? All I wanted was to sleep in my new, comfy bed and soak in the peace and quiet.

"I didn't know what else to do, she was freaking out and punched me," Maverick explains to one of them, I assume, whoever asked why he was here.

"Well, she's awake now, so I don't think you need to pin her down." Cooper points out.

His head snaps back to me, putting his face directly in front of mine, our noses brushing. I'm almost cross-eyed meeting his dark stare.

He pulls back just as quickly, making me hiss when his weight is finally lifted off me. I think I see a hint of remorse on his face at the sound before it's wiped away just as fast.

He lunges forward to help me when I struggle to sit up, Kai coming around the side of the bed to prop some of my pillows behind me.

The bed is a complete mess, pillows strewn all over it and the floor. The weighted comforter, as well as the sheets, are wrapped all around each other and completely pulled from each corner. The sheets are wrinkled and clearly fought with, and a quick touch tells me they're as soaked through with sweat as I am.

The four of them look back at me, waiting for anything to be said, but I'm still trying to piece together what happened.

I remember lying down and getting settled in the bed as best I could with the sling; the lights were out, but I was staring at the reflection of the fairy lights on the wall and ceiling. I must have drifted off quickly, and then flashes of the faceless man in my dorm started.

It felt real, I could feel all the blows, and the pain to the back of my skull as if it just happened.

Reality and my dream crossed over at some point, which is how I heard the guys yelling and how I ended up hitting Maverick.

"You were screaming pretty loud, Lottie. Are you okay?" Kai asks, sitting beside me in the bed, but being careful not to touch me.

My heart's still pounding in my chest, and I'm clammy and coated with sweat, but physically for the moment, I'm fine.

I ignore Maverick's eye roll when I nod my head, and even the rest of the guys give me skeptical looks in return. But I guess it's hard to argue with a mute.

"Okay, well, we should all try to get back to sleep. It's the middle of the night, and I know we're all tired." Cooper suggests, making his way out of the room, followed closely by Eli and Maverick.

Instead of getting settled in the bed, I shuffle to the edge, ready to stand and struggle my way through a shower. There's no way that I'll be able to rest feeling like this.

Kai hovers by my side, hands out like he's waiting to catch me if I fall, and the rest of the guys stay close by.

Moving into the bathroom, Kai stays by the door rather than following me in. I reach into the shower to start the water and let it warm up while I go in search of the things I'll need.

Turning around, Kai looks uncertain in the doorway. Just beyond him, I see the others peeking in with looks of concern.

"Do you really think you can manage getting in the shower right now?"

Nodding, I ignore Kai, stepping around him to look in the closet for a clean towel to use, and another one for my hair since it desperately needs a wash to get it out of the rat's nest state it's in on top of my head.

"Charlotte, you just got home, and you're tired," Cooper joins in, "Your doctor said that you won't be able to shower on your own, so if you can't wait until morning, then I need you to pick one of us to help you out here."

I give him a questioning look, wondering if he's serious.

Before he can answer, Kai inserts himself, sighing heavily before starting to pull off his shirt.

"Well, if someone's gotta do it, then I'll take one for the team." He shrugs, flexing his abs.

The sound of Cooper slapping him upside the head echoes around the room, making a laugh bubble up inside me, and he cringes.

Eli steps forward, "Charlie, I know you don't want to have help, but for our peace of mind, please just let us know who you're okay with having in here with you. It won't hurt anyone's feelings, but someone needs to be with you. You can't even raise your arm to get undressed right now with the sling."

Logically, I know they're right. I'm not very capable of doing things on my own at the moment, but it doesn't make it any easier. With all the doubts I'm having in my mind about the guys even wanting to be with me anymore, the thought of them seeing me undressed plants that seed of doubt even further, that maybe they won't like what they see, and it will just further prove the point that they don't want me. Plus, there are all the nerves that I've never been undressed with anyone before, and that's a whole other can of worms that I don't care to dive into.

Eli can say there'll be no hurt feelings with whoever I choose, but the reality is that someone will always feel left out at some point.

"I'll just do it, it's no big deal, and it will be fine." Kai jumps in when I don't respond.

"No, you're not going to steamroll the decision; it's her choice," Cooper argues.

"You can't just speak for her." Eli sides with Cooper.

"She can't speak right now, she's comfortable with me, I've helped her change before, it's the same difference!"

"It's not the same difference! And taking her choice away isn't okay!" Cooper retorts.

Their voices rise, talking over one another as they continue to argue over what I might want or what I might choose.

The sound of their bickering starts to grate on my nerves; overwhelmed by the varying opinions, the feeling of my clothes sticking to me makes me want to crawl out of my skin.

Looking for an escape, I look to the open doorway, finding Maverick there, leaning against the frame with his arms crossed and a pensive look on his face while he watches them argue.

It's odd not to see him step in the middle of them, but he's made his stance on our relationship clear in the past. I know he doesn't want a part of it, so I guess that means that he's going to stay out of it altogether.

"Maverick," The name slips out without thought, surprising everyone in the room, including myself.

Maverick's face changes instantly, shifting from passive to surprised as his eyes find mine, and the room falls silent.

"She talked," Kai whispers.

"No shit, we all heard her." Eli fires back.

"I know, but she said *Maverick*." Kai seems dumbfounded by my choice, and I honestly have to agree with him a little bit.

But now that I've said it, it makes sense. I have nothing to lose by asking Maverick to help me; there are no stakes. He doesn't want to be with me, and even if he's annoyed at me being a burden, or if he's disgusted with what he sees, there's no relationship being strained.

"Okay then, Mav, can you help her then?" Cooper asks him, rousing him from his perch in the doorway.

Maverick clears the shock from his face and steps into the room, nodding once and making room for them to leave.

Cooper gives me a reassuring smile before leaving the room with Eli close behind him without another word.

Kai hovers in front of me, reluctant to leave me in here.

"Are you sure?"

Refusing to go back on my choice or to backslide back into not speaking after forcing Maverick's name out, I square my shoulders.

Looking him directly in the eyes, I tell him, "Yes, I'm sure."

He hovers for a few more seconds, studying my face before relenting and stepping out of the room. The door shuts softly behind him, and I keep my eyes trained on the floor, nerves bubbling up now that I'm alone with Maverick.

It might be clear that he doesn't want a relationship with me, but that doesn't stop the feelings that I've had for him. Even as stand-offish and irritating as he is, butterflies erupt every time I find myself alone with him.

Without lifting my eyes, I watch him step around the room, grabbing clean towels, washcloths, some new body wash, and new bottles of shampoo and conditioner, lining all of them out on the counter before stopping in front of me.

He doesn't say anything and doesn't rush me, waiting quietly for me to get my racing heart to calm down.

Taking a chance, I glance up. His eyes are almost black, staring back at me. I cave quickly, opting to look at his chest instead.

"I'll just help you get undressed down to your underwear like last time, and then I'll stand in the shower with you to help. Just let me know when you're ready."

I've never heard his voice so soft before; it's a complete contrast to the usual annoyed tone he uses with me. I don't think I would have ever guessed that he has a soft side.

I imagine that by 'last time' he's referring to when I was sick and out of my mind. I only have snippets of him forcing me into a cold shower, but I have no real recollection of how that went.

I nod, but he doesn't let me off that easily, dipping down to my level to catch my eyes.

"Does that mean you're ready?" His mouth curves up at the side, softening the blow of his callout.

Rolling my eyes, I give him what he wants.

"Yes, I'm r-ready." Cursing myself for the stutter coming out, showing my nerves externally, I breathe a quick sigh of relief when he starts to move.

I can't do much to help, I just watch as he carefully undoes the Velcro that holds the sling strap together, letting it slip through the rings until he can slip it off my arm. His hand circles my forearm, keeping my arm bent and close to my side where it's been resting.

He lets go, holding his hands over my arm like he's silently telling me to keep it there while he moves to grab the hem of my shirt.

I hold my breath as he starts to pull it up and over my head, bracing myself for any type of reaction from him. A quick look at his face only shows me intense concentration as he navigates slipping the shirt down and off my bad shoulder and arm.

It was a struggle and a half for the nurse to help me slip on a light bra this morning, so I'm already dreading taking it off, and I'm thankful for the time in the shower to postpone that experience.

Once my upper body is free, Maverick makes quick work of shedding my sweat pants, leaving me in my very plain black bra and boy shorts.

Before I can blink, he strips his shirt and pants in one quick swoop, leaving him in skin-tight, black compression shorts with his broad chest bare and on display, inches from my face. It's mesmerizing to look at the way the black ink on his skin stands out against his tan complexion, making it look three-dimensional. I want to reach out and touch it to see how it feels, but I barely manage to resist the urge.

Keeping one hand on my arm, he leads me over to the shower; luckily, it's a walk-in, so I don't have to worry about him having to help me step in and potentially embarrassing myself further.

Stepping into the stream, I instantly start to relax, and I just soak in the warmth as the hot water rolls over me and melts away the sweat and lingering feeling from the hospital that's been clinging to my skin.

He jumps back the second he steps behind me, and the water touches his skin.

“Shit!”

Looking over my shoulder, I see him standing in the far corner of the shower, looking horrified.

“What?”

“That water is hotter than Satan’s asshole!” He looks horrified, “How the hell are you standing in it without catching fire?”

“It’s not even that hot; it feels good.” Are all guys this dramatic when it comes to the water temperature in the shower? I thought some people said it was fun to shower together, but I think they might be confused.

“It’s hot enough that I’m afraid my skin is going to start melting off before we’re done.” He mutters under his breath, lathering the washcloth with bodywash and pulling me out of the water towards him.

Starting on my good side, he washes from my shoulder, down my arm, and then across my shoulder blades before sweeping around my torso.

“Let me know if I’m hurting anything.” He warns just seconds before his hand lands on my bad shoulder.

It doesn’t feel great, but he’s handling it with such care and clinical precision that it’s not unbearable. When he skims my collarbone, he uses such a featherlight touch that if I weren’t watching, I wouldn’t have even noticed it.

I focus on his face now that he's too busy to catch me. His eyebrows are furrowed in concentration, and sparks of anger flash in his eyes each time he passes over a patch of discolored skin.

He slides down to his knees, and butterflies erupt in my stomach, making me lightheaded. I have to catch myself on his shoulders when I sway, earning me a sharp look from him, and oh holy hell, the shower is starting to feel a bit too hot now.

You know, I've read about men kneeling before a woman before in some spicy romance books, and I never understood the appeal. That is, until a beast of a man like Maverick Locke is in front of you, looking up with flushed cheeks, wet hair, and his piercing green eyes.

I need to get a hold of myself; it is ridiculous to react like this because of *Maverick*. He hates me, and yet I'm melting into a puddle because of how he looks on his knees. That thought alone is ridiculous. I'm sure the last thing going through his mind is something along those lines. He's here because he feels obligated; I'm his brother's girlfriend, and I got hurt, and then, in a pathetic act of stupidity, I asked him to be the one to help me instead of one of said boyfriends. All because I'm too scared to show my boyfriends my body, the joke is on me because even though I chose Maverick to help, I'm still worried about what he might be thinking, looking at my unimpressive frame.

I can't seem to win here.

I just need this to be over as soon as possible so I can run and hide myself away in my room and wait for the embarrassment to smother me alive and put me out of my misery.

9

~ Maverick~

I swear I was a saint in another life.

There's no other explanation as to how I have found the willpower to avoid looking at any of the unmentionable parts of Charlotte that have become visible since stepping into the shower.

Well, I may have glanced, but I didn't linger, and she didn't notice.

She manages to catch herself on my shoulders while I work on washing her legs. Looking up at her, I'm met with wide eyes and a flushed face. Something tells me that's not from the water temperature.

I haven't had a chance to talk with her since she woke up, so I have no idea if she has any recollection of what I told her back in her dorm. My gut says no, but that doesn't mean all hope is lost for me. It's clear to see that she holds feelings for me.

Not just in the way that her body is reacting from being in the shower with me, or the way that her cheeks flush rosy pink every time I push her buttons. She chose me to help her tonight. Either completely on a whim or because deep down she knows she can trust me, it doesn't matter.

I know my brothers are pissed, and they probably don't understand why she'd ask for me, but it's not a competition; it's whatever she needs. They're all quick to preach about it until it conflicts with what they want, and that's what tends to stress her out. I watched her earlier, standing in the middle of them while they bickered like children. The discomfort was written all over her face, and the way she fidgeted with her hands was a clear sign she was freaking out inside.

I'm glad she asked for me, even if it means I'm fighting to keep myself composed right now.

Seeing the bruises all over her skin without the coverage of her baggy clothes or the sling has me burning up with rage.

The bruises are so dark, all of them forming together like a roadmap to show how that motherfucker let loose on her. All of them are reminders that whoever he is, he's still out there, and that we have no clue why this happened.

It's enough to make me want to drive my fist through the wall. Especially the finger-shaped bruises around her throat, the ones that silenced her when I was on the other end of the phone. The ones that kept her voice from us for days, until she finally found it tonight. She thought she could go back to not speaking after finding her voice to call to me, but she was sorely mistaken if she thought I'd let her retreat back into her shell like that.

She hasn't moved the whole time I've been washing her, other than when I've moved her. Her arm is still stiff by her side, where I told her to keep it, so she at least isn't stubborn enough to fight me on that.

Standing back up, I'm careful to keep my eyes anywhere but on her soaked bra, which is fully transparent at this point.

Her eyes are trained on my chest, which is normal for her, but I watch as she follows different water droplets as they race down my pecs, looking up to find new ones when they leave her field of view.

"Did you want your hair washed?" She jumps at the sound of my voice, the blush in her cheeks darkening as she realizes I was watching her.

Biting her lip, she nods.

I cock an eyebrow, waiting for her to use her words.

"P-please. If i-it's not too much work." Her stutter slips out, a dead giveaway that she's nervous.

Turning her around, I let her enjoy the fiery water while I work on pulling her hair out of what once was a bun on top of her head. Now it resembles more of a bird's nest, and I'm struggling to see where it starts.

When I hesitate too long to make a move, she reaches up with her good hand, blindly grabbing the rubber band and pulling on it.

I've seen her do it before; normally, it slides right out of her hair, but this time it gets stuck, resulting in her yanking on her hair and only managing to free one or two strands at a time.

Finally, I make myself move, pushing her hand away and carefully untangling the strands until it all falls down around her shoulders in different states of frizz and knots.

I see her shoulders move more than I hear her huff. I can practically see her rolling her eyes at my quick dismissal of her assistance.

She doesn't fidget at all with her back turned to me, though; she does start to sway some as my fingers rub and scratch at her scalp. She seems to enjoy the feeling of her hair being washed, and I have to wonder if that's something that my brothers know. I hardly ever see them initiate any type of contact with her, other than hugging her, which is evident she doesn't like, but I wonder if they've ever tried to find anything she does like, or if they're just content to leave the ball in her court.

If that's what they're doing, then my guess is they're going to be waiting a hell of a long time.

I use the hand attachment on the showerhead to rinse all the shampoo out of her hair, combing out the knots with my fingers as I go.

"What are you doing?" Her voice almost startles me with its unexpectedness as I grab the conditioner bottle.

"I washed it, now it needs conditioner," I tell her, confused why she's asking.

"Do you use conditioner?"

"No." I'm confused where her question is coming from, but rather than offer up anything more, I wait. I lather the long locks, make sure the ends are covered, and then comb it all through with my fingers.

She doesn't make me wait long. "How do you know to use it then?"

It's such an innocent question, but it draws a laugh from me before I can stop it.

"I might not have long hair, but I've had girlfriends before. They used to complain anytime they forgot their conditioner, but needed to wash their hair."

"Oh," I see her shoulders stiffen for a moment at the mention of my having girlfriends, but she recovers quickly, relaxing back into the feeling of hot water rinsing her hair.

I haven't had a chance to talk to her about my feelings, but at least I can catch the signs that she feels something for me. That, combined with how much the twins didn't blink an eye when I told them I wanted in.

I'll have to man up and have that talk with her soon, rather than let her go on thinking I hate her. But for tonight, I'll call this shower enough progress.

As much as I'm sure Charlotte would love to stand here and boil under the water for awhile, I'm sweating my ass off with the steam and she's starting to sway more now, probably the exhaustion sweeping back in to claim her shortly. She doesn't protest when I reach around to shut the water off, but I also don't miss her lower lip sticking out into a pout at the loss of warmth.

I wrap a towel around my waist and grab another to hold out for her as she steps out. I wrap one around her and another around her hair so we can tackle getting her dressed, which I'm hoping will go more smoothly than last time.

Kai stuck his head in while we were showering to drop off another set of clothes for her, so those wait on the counter as I work out how to get her sports bra off without hurting her shoulder.

"How attached are you to that bra?" I ask, watching her cheeks flush dark crimson, and her face falls into a mask of confusion.

"W-what?"

I snap the strap against her good shoulder, "The bra, are you going to be devastated if I cut it?"

"N-no, but w-why do you n-need to cut it?"

"Because as tedious as it was for the nurse to get on this morning, it's probably going to take twice as long to get it off with it being wet. That and I can't promise it won't hurt trying to peel it off without bothering your collarbone or your wrist."

I can see the puzzle pieces snap together right in front of me. Her bewildered expression gives way, and understanding shines through.

"It's fine, w-whatever is easiest."

With her blessing, I grab the scissors and cut straight through the back, making sure the towel is tucked around her front so she's not exposed.

With very little help from her, I manage to reach under the towel to guide the remnants of the bra down her good arm and then off her bad shoulder with minimal cringing on her part.

She keeps a death grip on the towel as I make quick work of shedding her underwear, then I make myself look busy by getting rid of the torn garment so she can have a moment to dry the rest of the way.

She refuses to make eye contact as I slip a t-shirt over her head and arms, then dress her in a fresh pair of underwear and sweats, finally letting her drop the towel to her feet.

She lets me towel-dry and brush her hair before slipping the sling back around her to support her arm.

No words are shared as I move around her, but it seems to be a comfortable silence and a form of communication between the two of us as she agrees to everything I need her to do to help me help her.

She doesn't even protest when I grab a brand new hair brush from one of the drawers and set to work brushing out her hair. Her only commentary comes when I start pulling her hair back to braid, layering the strands over and under each other.

"Where'd you learn to braid?" I have to straighten her head back when she tilts it to the side, watching me over her shoulder in the mirror.

"My mom always wanted a daughter. When she ended up with all boys, she said that we had to do girly stuff with her so she didn't 'drown in the testosterone'." I can't fight the smile pulling at my lips at the memory of her. "That meant learning to braid hair, paint nails, cooking, baking, and even rom-com movie nights."

She laughs, and it's the most magical sound I've ever heard. Her face shines brightly in the mirror as she smiles with ease. This is one of the first times I've seen her look truly young and carefree, not riddled with anxiety.

"I'm sure you *loved* that." Another giggle breaks free, and I can't help but join in.

"Maybe not so much at the time," I admit. "But it's some of my favorite memories I have with her. And it seems to be coming in handy now."

Tying off the braid, I'm reluctant to burst this little bubble we've found ourselves in. But she needs to sleep, and I don't have any other excuses for keeping her in here.

Opening the door, I gesture for her to go first, and I follow a step behind her to her room.

Stepping over the threshold, she stops in her tracks.

The bed is now freshly made with new sheets, looking much more put-together than before. I think her shock is more about the two men residing on the floor on either side of the bed. Kai and Eli are both passed out asleep on homemade cots, ready to spring into action if she has another nightmare.

I make a mental note to ask her what it was about sometime.

I step over Kai, pulling the blankets back for her.

"It seems you're in good hands." When she doesn't make a move to get into bed, I add, "I can kick them out of here if it makes you uncomfortable."

"N-no, it's fine." She shakes her head, stepping carefully over to the bed and sliding in as best she can with the sling. I help her settle in, moving pillows around to support her arm and moving the blankets until she's comfortable.

Her eyes begin to droop as she fades quickly. Unable to help myself, I lean forward, brushing a kiss against her forehead.

"Sleep tight," I whisper, but her eyes remain closed.

I quietly retreat from the room, pulling the door shut behind me, knowing that the twins can take it from here, but also hating the small part of me that wants to turn around and scoop her up to hide her away in my room so nothing else can hurt her.

I'm not ready for that, and I know she's not, not until we talk at the very least.

Tonight was at least a step, hopefully in the right direction.

10

~ Charlotte ~

It's been about a week of living with the guys, and so far, the weirdest part of it all is how Maverick seems to have turned into a normal human being overnight.

Rather than the typical harsh asshole I've come to know, he's been a kind and, dare I say, funny person to be around. He hasn't been keeping himself holed up in his office day and night like the other times I've been around him. It seems he's making a valid effort to be around everyone outside of his walks with Zeus and his personal time in the gym.

The guys still take shifts in watching me, never leaving me on my own for longer than an hour at most. It's nice, but it's also starting to put me a bit on edge.

I'm a creature of habit, and my habits consist of programming and gaming alone in my room and surviving on a diet of crappy noodles and energy drinks. I used to only socialize when I had to leave my room for lectures and the occasional dreaded grocery run.

They've all hovered over me as if they don't have eyes on me, then I'll disappear. At first, I was just confused, thinking they all thought I was going to run off or maybe even hurt myself. Now I've come to know it's more about the fear they all felt on Christmas when they got the call from Maverick, and it's the only way they can try to process it all.

I've enjoyed spending time with them, playing video games, watching movies, or just sitting and watching Maverick cook for us every night, but the closer we get to going back to classes and work, the more my anxiety starts to ramp up.

Not knowing who attacked me makes me fear going out and being around a bunch of strangers intensify even more. My heart races each time I think that any person I encounter at school or on the street could be the one who almost took my life.

My mind is also racing, wondering how far I could be in my search for Ivy if I weren't attacked. I was making good progress leading up to that night, and I had plans laid out for everything else I needed to start digging into, but that's all on my hard drive, which is back in my dorm.

I briefly mentioned to Kai that I wanted to go back and grab it, but he was firmly against the idea, saying I didn't need to see the aftermath. The idea of sitting around and doing nothing while she was still missing made me sick to my stomach, though.

I haven't even had access to a computer since coming home with the guys. Something about my concussion and not being allowed on screens.

I don't think they understand that not having the comfort of a computer will do me more harm than good.

The door behind me opens, interrupting the silence I'd been soaking in. I've been out here on the back patio for just about an hour, so it was right on schedule for someone to come find me.

I'd been watching Zeus dig holes in the yard, something that Maverick got pissed about every time, but he looked like he was having fun.

"Maverick's going to be pissed." Eli snorts behind me, coming to sit on the couch beside me.

I watch Zeus jump out of the hole he's been working on and into a fresh patch of grass to start another, his tail wagging a mile a minute.

"Maverick will live, it's just grass."

"Grass that took him all of last summer trying to get perfectly even and in shape."

Shit, I didn't think about the fact that Maverick put work into making the yard look how he wanted. Like a dark cloud forming over my head, my enjoyment of watching Zeus is zapped, replaced with that feeling of dread bubbling in my gut at his reaction.

I look down and see myself twisting my fingers, something I haven't done in over a week, but it seems I can still manage even with the sling on.

"Z-zeus, c-c-come," I call out, his attention instantly on me as he runs over to sit with his head on my lap.

Sensing the shift in mood, Eli turns to face me, covering my hands with his to halt my fidgeting.

"Hey, it's no big deal. Maverick knows he digs. I think he likes to act more annoyed than he really is just for something to complain about."

I know he's right, but I can't stop my heart from pounding or my palms from sweating.

Faking a smile, I try to get Eli to stop watching me like a hawk. Maybe if I can convince him I'm okay, then my body will start to believe it too.

I can tell by his face that he's not buying it, but luckily for my sake, he pretends to go along with it.

"So, what are you doing out here all by yourself?" His thumb rubs aimlessly along the back of my hand, giving me something to focus on as I try to quiet the buzzing noise in my head.

"I just n-needed some fresh air."

I watch his thumb, moving back and forth, over and over again, counting the passes, and I feel my heart start to slow down.

"Starting to feel a little stir crazy?" He asks.

"Yeah, I can only listen to Kai quote The Office so many times in an afternoon before I need a break."

"Well, let's get out of here," He suggests, "Anywhere you want to go?"

Leave it to Eli to lay out my golden opportunity to get my hard drive without Maverick knowing and catching on to what I want to work on.

"I a-actually wanted to stop by my d-dorm." His thumb stops in place on my hand, his eyes searching mine while he thinks.

"For what? I thought Cooper and Kai got what you needed when they stopped by before you came home."

"Just my hard drive, I w-want to use the computers in my room, b-but they didn't know to look for the drive on my desk."

His thumb starts to move again, giving me something to focus on while he contemplates my request. I notice his leg starts to bounce as well, reminding me of the dream I had while I was in the hospital, when I saw his nervous tics.

"Are you sure? Kai said it was bad when he stopped there. Do you really want to see that?"

I get they're trying to protect me from seeing the aftermath and getting upset, but all of them are making that decision for me and not giving me a chance to choose how to deal with this, and that's what is starting to drive me crazy.

Seeing my room destroyed is going to hurt, piss me off, and possibly bring up even more memories of that night. But regardless, I will get over it if it means I can get the stupid hard drive and get to work on finding Ivy.

Whatever discomfort I'm going to suffer from just from seeing my room is nothing compared to what I imagine Ivy might be going through right now.

"It'll be fine, I already know what it looks like. I was there after all." I remind him.

"Yeah," His eyes darken, "Don't remind me."

Biting my tongue, I refrain from saying anything else to irritate him. My desire to get back to work has me forgetting how sensitive a topic that night is for the guys.

I brace myself for his denial, preparing for whatever excuse he gives for not wanting to take me, but then he surprises me.

"Alright, we can go. But if Maverick finds out, I'll deny it. You can deal with his temper tantrum."

"I don't know, he seems different the last couple of days, not as grumpy."

Standing up, he helps me off the couch and back inside.

"If you say so."

The house seems quiet as we make our way out. Cooper and Maverick went into the office today for a few hours, and Kai is on grocery duty this week, so he's been out for a couple of hours.

Eli leads me to his blacked-out charger, opening the door for me and giving me flashbacks to our first date not long ago. It feels like ages ago now, and I never thought that I'd start to feel as comfortable around them as I do now. It's terrifying to think how much they've intertwined their lives with mine, thinking about how much power it gives them over me. If they decide this relationship is too much for them, I fear it will break me beyond what I can handle. But at the same time, the feeling of having someone close, to count on, is exciting. It's a very double-edged sword that I still haven't been able to wrap my mind around.

Eli's playlist filters through the speakers, filling the car with the soft sounds of Hear You Me by Jimmy Eat World.

The traffic today is heavy, all the out-of-towners heading back home now that the holidays have passed, making our fifteen-minute drive more like forty minutes. I don't mind; the silence with Eli isn't uncomfortable, and neither one of us tries to fill it with pointless small talk. He's just as content to be together as I am.

"How's your arm feeling?" He asks, eyeing me fidgeting with a string that's come loose on the strap.

"My wrist isn't very sore anymore. I can actually hold things in my hand now."

Nodding, he drums his fingers on the wheel, inching forward another twenty feet in the traffic.

"That's good. You only have to wear the sling for another couple weeks, right?"

“I think. I’m supposed to go back to see the doctor next week to check.”

The song shifts into another popular track from the Goo Goo Dolls, both of us falling silent again as we hum along.

Soon enough, the traffic gives way, and we’re pulling up to my dorm. Shutting off the car, we both sit for a moment, staring at the front doors.

“Are you sure you want to go in?” He asks, “You can just tell me where the drive is, and I can grab it.”

Now that we’re here, there’s a pit in my stomach swirling with all the flashes of memories I have of the man in my room, raining blows down on me and choking me out. My palms sweat as my hands shake at the thought of going back in there, but I’ve come this far, and I feel like I need to see it so I can move forward. Maybe just to remind myself that all of it really happened and that my brain didn’t conjure up these nightmares on its own.

“No, it’s f-fine. Let’s j-just do it.” Without giving him any room to argue, I open the door and awkwardly climb out.

We’re still on break, so the campus is deserted. The halls echo our steps with no other noise to drown them out.

Reaching my dorm, the evidence of that night is immediate. The door barely hangs on the hinges, signs of Maverick kicking it in from where it’d been barricaded with a barstool.

Ripping the band-aid off, I push it open. All the air is sucked from my lungs at seeing the state of everything.

Broken glass still litters the floor, along with shattered furniture. My bed is bare, no longer covered with my weighted blankets, and my computer monitors both still sit on the desk with cracked screens.

The glass crunches beneath my feet as I carefully move through the room, stopping suddenly when I see the dried blood on the floor. In that moment, I can feel his hands around my neck again as my lungs scream for air. I sense the pulsating pain at the back of my skull from where he slammed it against the floor, and I feel the ache in my collarbone from when it cracked after being slammed to the ground.

I can hear my accelerating heart rate pounding in my ears, and it becomes much harder to breathe. I want to reach up and pry the hands off my neck, but they're not real, and I'm paralyzed, stuck watching my nightmare replay in my mind.

"Charlie!" Eli's voice brings my mind to a screeching halt, the images before me clearing instantly, and the phantom hands around my throat are gone. The only thing I see is Eli's face inches from mine as she shakes my shoulders, trying to pull me out of the trance.

"S-s-sorry." I choke out between gulps of air.

"What the hell, you scared the shit out of me. You were like somewhere else; you wouldn't respond to anything I was saying."

Shaking his hands off, I step around him to get to my desk. Avoiding looking at anything else in the room, I've seen what I needed to see. I just want to grab the hard drive and get the hell out of here.

With a trembling hand, I reach around the back of the desk, where I have the drive nestled in the frame, and pull the wires out one by one. I grab the drive, pulling it free from the desk.

Ignoring Eli's strained expression, I side-step him to escape the room, not looking back.

That room was my safe haven for nearly four years, the first place I truly felt content after escaping my parents' control. Now, it's nothing more than an empty shell filled with broken pieces of who I was before the guys entered my life. I'm determined not to revert to that shy and timid person, so that room holds no meaning for me anymore. I don't want to see any of the memories the walls hold, especially not from the last night I was here, hiding from the men who make me feel alive. I won't keep running from what could make me happy just to find comfort in my familiar space.

Eli falls into step beside me, not saying a word as we hightail it out of the building and back to his car. Again, he opens the door for me, helping me get settled before taking his spot.

Only once we're both settled, and the car is running, does he break the silence.

"So, I'm glad that's over." He forces a laugh, trailing off when I don't join in. "Let's do something more enjoyable. Want to go get something sweet?"

Smiling, I nod. I'm thankful that he's not pushing the minor panic attack I had back in the dorm, or the way that I'm clearly avoiding talking about what caused it, even after I insisted that I'd be fine seeing the dorm.

I know I'll have to open up and talk about it at some point, but for now, it's so much easier to push it down and pretend it's not a big deal.

Denial was always my parents' favorite method of problem-solving…

11

~ Eli ~

The drive to Jeremiah's gives me time to get my heart rate under control again.

I don't experience anxiety much, but watching Charlie have a panic attack has me spiraling.

The way she stopped dead in her tracks, pale-faced and gasping for air, was terrifying to see, especially when I realized there was nothing I could do to help her. I had to just wait for her to snap out of it. I don't think there's a much worse feeling than being helpless, and that's all I've felt like since she woke up in the hospital.

She picked Maverick to help her with showering, which shocked all of us. Kai and her play video games together, Cooper watches movies with her every night, and I'm left floating in the background. I don't feel there's much I can specifically help her with. The one thing I'm good at doing, she's been banned from for the last week.

That's why today, when she asked to go get her hard drive, I couldn't say no. This was my one opportunity to be useful, and selfishly, I thought that if she got her hard drive, then she'd be inclined to work on some code, and that maybe we could do that together, so I could spend time with her like my brothers.

I didn't think the trip to her dorm was a good idea, and I guess I was right. But on the bright side, now it's done and over with, and we can do something fun instead. Though I am curious to see what was so important on the hard drive that it made Charlie want to face her demons to get it.

We pull up to the familiar green and orange building, somewhere I've been coming since I was a kid. Dad used to take the four of us out for Italian ice every Sunday after dinner for 'boys bonding time', it's some of the earliest memories I have since being adopted into the family, and something I miss more than anything else in the world.

I'm happy to bring Charlie here to create new memories in a place that once brought me so much joy. And if I'm lucky, she'll have the same fondness for this place as I do.

She hasn't said a word since we left the dorm, and I don't know if she's still reeling from the panic attack or if she's just content to be here with me.

I pry the hard drive out of her hand, putting it in the center console so she sees that it's in a safe place before getting out to open her door. I even take a chance and grab her good hand in mine, waiting for the usual rejection to come and for her to pull away. She surprises me when she doesn't; instead, she grips my hand tightly in hers.

She takes an impossible amount of time to pick from the massive menu board, but I'm not in any rush. It gives me time to watch her as she reads over the options over and over again, biting her lip while she tries to make her choice.

In the end, she chooses a peanut butter and jelly flavored ice layered with vanilla soft serve, an interesting choice, but I'm not one to judge. I stick to my usual mint ice and chocolate ice cream.

We pick a table off in the corner of the lot, giving a semblance of privacy and an opportunity to watch the cars drive by as we eat.

Charlie takes her first bite, getting a scoop of jelly-flavored ice, and I watch her eyes roll back into her head as she savors the taste, a small moan escaping her lips, making my jeans tighten in the process.

"Good?" I ask, subtly shifting in my seat.

Licking her lips, she nods, diving in for another bite.

It makes me laugh, watching her eat each individual layer, but it's even more comical to see her horrified expression as I stir mine with my spoon, blending all the flavors together before taking a bite.

"What? It's supposed to be mixed together; that way, you get the intended flavor."

"But how can you savor all of the flavors when they're mixed together like that?" She still looks slightly disturbed, but continues to dig in.

“Agree to disagree, I guess.” I admit, not wanting to make fun of her quirks. I’ve noticed, especially over the past week, that she has a unique way of approaching food. She doesn’t like her food to touch, except for certain dishes where she permits it. She also eats everything one item at a time. She’s not the type to take a bite of a burger, then a bite of fries; she eats all of her fries first, then moves on to the burger. With ice cream, she’ll pick out any add-ins before eating the ice cream itself. It’s cute to watch and just another thing that makes her special. Overall, it’s amazing how much I’ve learned just by living under the same roof.

“So,” I don’t want to kill the mood, but I also want a chance to talk to her before we get home and have anyone else eavesdropping on us. “What’s so important on the hard drive that you *had* to go get it?”

Her spoon freezes mid-air. I see her gulp as she becomes fascinated with her food.

“J-just some files I have saved f-for jobs that I’ve worked. I d-didn’t want to lose t-them.”

I don’t buy it. Her stuttering alone clues me into the fact that she’s not telling the truth. She only stutters when she’s nervous or when she’s not telling the whole truth. Why is the question?

“If it were for old jobs, why does it matter if you have access to the files or not?”

She shrugs, “It’s supposed to b-be c-confidential.”

"But no one even knew the drive was there. Even when they went to clean out your dorm, it most likely would have been trashed. Who do you think would have dug into it?"

She doesn't try to come up with anything this time, opting to just shrug, pushing away the rest of her cup to twist her fingers.

Setting my own cup aside, I level with her. I don't want to push her, but she's clearly hiding something, and after what's already happened, the last thing I want is her putting herself in another situation to get hurt.

"Whatever it is, just tell me. I won't get mad, and I won't throw a fit. I'm not Maverick." The joke falls flat, "I just don't want you diving into anything alone. I'm here for you."

She remains silent; time stretches on as she watches the cars pass, twisting and pulling at her fingers like a lifeline. Just as I'm about to give in and take her home, she heaves a sigh, meeting my eyes for just a moment.

"After Maverick t-turned Ivy's case over t-to JSO, I kept l-looking." She admits, refusing to look at me. "I have f-files saved, p-places where she might be. I c-can't drop the case."

That makes so much sense. I remember how pissed she was at Mav when he demanded she hand over the case. She spent weeks not talking to him because of the way he tried to just throw her work away, deeming it too much for us to handle. I get why she needed the drive so badly now, and I also get why she'd ask me, of all of us, to go and get it. I know how it feels to be knee-deep into a case, feeling like the answers you need might just be in reach, and to get shut down right when the trail is hot.

"So that's what you've been doing in all your free time leading up to Christmas?" I'm not blind; she was burnt out and exhausted in the weeks that we started going out. For days at a time, if we didn't have plans, she was practically radio silent until one of us checked in on her.

She nods.

"And I take it that no one knows about your little side quest?"

The guilt written all over her face answers for her.

This just became much more interesting, and a nagging voice in the back of my mind wonders if it has anything to do with why she was attacked. Without seeing what information she has and what exactly she was looking into, though, I won't know.

Mav will have an aneurysm if he finds out what she's been up to. She trusts me enough to admit it, and I won't be the one to crush that trust. If this does have anything to do with her attacker, then I want to be by her side, protecting her from anything else that could hurt her. I won't shut her down the way that Mav does, but that doesn't mean I'll turn a blind eye.

"Okay."

I grab both our cups, toss them in the trash, and offer her a hand back to the car. She stares at it, dumbfounded, only following when I reach out and take hers.

"T-that's it?" She stops me from shutting the car door once I get her settled in, searching my face for any signs of lies.

Crouching down, I put myself on her level, making sure I have her full attention.

"I won't tell anyone," Relief washes over her, all that pent-up anxiety rolling off her in waves, but her walls shoot right back up at my next words. "But I'm not going to let you do this alone. If you want to keep looking into Ivy's disappearance, then you can…as long as I can help you."

"Why?"

Tilting my head, I wonder what she's asking.

"Why do you want to go against your brother to help me?"

Ah, she doesn't yet realize that any of the four of us would do nearly anything she asked, without hesitation. She doesn't understand the pull she has on all of us, but eventually she'll come to see it.

Because you're not alone. You might not realize it yet, but we're here for you—all of us. Plus, two sets of eyes are always better than one, and after all the effort you've put in, I believe you're close to figuring it out. I just want to be there to support you through it.

With no other objections, I jump into the car, taking us home so we can dive headfirst into the case that she's willing to risk it all for.

I just hope we can pull it off before Mav catches wind of what we're up to.

That would be the meltdown of the century.

12

~ Charlotte ~

Another week passes by, and things are finally starting to feel normal, or at least as normal as they can be.

Living with the guys, we've fallen into a comfortable routine. They aren't nearly as overbearing now that Maverick and Cooper have returned to the office every day, unable to stay home with new projects to work on.

Kai, Eli, and I have started our last semester of college. I opted to take my classes online, not able to fathom being around so many people. I didn't tell them about my plans to study online until the last minute, meaning that it was too late for Kai and Eli to take the same option. It means that I get some alone time while they attend classes. The peaceful silence is familiar to me, and I hate to admit that I've missed it quite a bit.

My classes are a breeze, full of information that I've taught myself years ago at this point, so I fly through them and give myself plenty of time to jump back into Ivy's case without any prying eyes.

There's plenty of time to work on it alone, seeing as Maverick deemed I'm not yet allowed back at work. I wanted to fight him on it, strictly on the principle that he shouldn't feel he can boss me around, but I knew that I had other priorities, so I didn't protest.

Eli's stuck to his word, not telling any of the others what I'm up to and helping me when he gets the chance, but it hasn't been much with school and work in the way for him. I feel bad about lying to the others, but I know that they'll stand in my way and throw away all my progress, and I'm not willing to give up on this right now.

Having access to a computer again has brought me a sense of peace that I've been missing since waking up. This is my comfort zone and where my mind feels most at peace. When my fingers fly across the keys, all the noise in my head comes to a screeching halt, allowing me to exist without the added stress of pretending to be 'normal'.

It's taken me a while to sort through all the files I had saved on the hard drive, reviewing and reorganizing everything so it all makes sense again, and I can have a good idea of where I need to go from here.

I have a list of potential buyers who viewed Ivy's listing that I found on the dark web, and I've spent a couple of days digging into each of them now that I've installed all my old software on this new setup. Finding the original post led me to cross-referencing it with the list of names to see who actually pursued the listing, and I feel like I'm close to uncovering who placed bids and maybe even who won the auction, if it's even happened yet.

I've also been trying and failing to get the software to run the footage from the bar the night that Ivy was there. It only ramps up my frustration every time I start to get images to cross-match IDs, and then a corrupted error fills the screen. This could go so much faster if I could just find the guy she left with that night, but it's a dead end every time I try.

A glance at the clock tells me I've been at this for way longer than I thought. The guys should be due home in less than an hour.

Figuring now's a good enough time to call it a day, I save my work and shut everything off, hoping my irritation will ease off before they get home.

Walking downstairs, I'm met with a mess from the night before. Blankets strewn all over the living room, shoes in the front hall by the door, and dishes from dinner littering the kitchen. The clutter makes my skin crawl; everything feels out of place.

Zeus perks up as I stomp into the kitchen, determined to clean up and feel less on edge. He watches from his bed as I start piling dirty dishes on the counter next to the sink, filling up one side with hot, soapy water.

This would be much easier with two hands, but I still have the damn sling on for at least another two weeks.

It takes an embarrassing amount of time to get the dishes washed, and half the water in the sink ends up on my shirt because of the awkwardness of having only one hand.

Not able to dry them, I stack them all in the drying rack, hating how it makes the kitchen look even more cluttered, even while being cleaner.

Giving up, I head into the living room, grabbing all the blankets into one pile to fold. But again, I'm met with the challenge of not being able to complete the simple task of folding a damn blanket.

Frustration boils inside me as I'm left with them all piled in front of me.

I straighten the pillows instead, to feel like I've done something productive, quickly abandoning this task to go back into the kitchen again.

The dishes may be clean, but the stove is splattered with grease, the counters and the floor are full of crumbs. I find a bottle of cleaner under the sink and grab a sponge as well. I scrub the stove, wiping every drop until I can see myself in the reflection. I knock all the crumbs from the counter onto the floor before repeating the process with the cleaner.

The kitchen smells strongly of lemon, but I still feel dirty.

I grab the broom from the hall closet, setting it against the wall so I can grab a bottle of water. The second I open the fridge, though, I see takeout containers with food that's definitely no good anymore. Grabbing those, I stack them on the counter, finding bottles of expired condiments and overly ripe vegetables too, adding them to the pile.

Leaving the pile, I grab the broom and awkwardly sweep the floor. Somehow, I manage to get them all swept and into the dustpan. Opening a new trash bag, I lay it out so I can dump the dustpan into it, then start throwing the pile from the fridge into the bag as well.

I drag the bag over to the door, leaving it there to get later.

Some of the dishes have dried enough to be put away, so I put them back in their place one by one. I've just picked up a coffee mug from the stack when a voice speaks out behind me.

"Charlotte?"

Jumping a foot into the air, the mug slips from my grasp, shattering on the floor and sending pieces of ceramic in every direction.

Blood rushes in my ears as my pounding heart starts to slow down, seeing it's Maverick who called out to me.

Looking back at the broken mug, my blood runs hot. Now the floor needs to be swept again.

Sights set on the broom, I notice the water I grabbed earlier. Snatching it up, I spin back to the fridge to put it back before sweeping again.

I can hear the mug crunching under my feet, but I don't feel anything as I stalk across the kitchen, swinging the door open more violently than I intend to put the bottle back. Slamming it shut, I spin around and slam into a wall of muscle.

Maverick's hands shoot out to steady me before I'm knocked to the floor, halting me in place.

His eyes bore into mine, his familiar scowl in place.

"What are you doing?" He demands.

"Cleaning." As if that wasn't obvious. I try to shrug off his hold, the urge to sweep up the mug intensifying, like an itch that needs to be scratched.

He doesn't budge, keeping me rooted in place.

"I can see that. Why are you cleaning?"

"Because I need to." Struggling in his hold, I try to shake him off, failing miserably.

The more he keeps me pinned down, the more frantic I get. I feel like a thousand ants are crawling all over my skin, taking over my body, and they're determined to drive me crazy if I don't finish what I started.

"Charlotte?" Cooper's voice sounds from the entryway. He looks around the kitchen, confusion etched into his face as he takes in the broken mug, trash, and Maverick holding me in place, unbothered by my struggles. "What are you doing?"

"She was *cleaning*," Maverick answers for me when I don't respond.

He studies the two of us, looking down at the floor.

"You're bleeding." He points out.

Following his gaze, I see drops of blood on the floor, a small puddle forming beneath my foot and coating several pieces of broken ceramic.

The sight of it makes my head spin, and flashbacks to the blood on my dorm floor make my stomach churn. I sway in Maverick's hold, suddenly feeling lightheaded.

He reacts instantly, swooping down to lift me up, depositing me on the counter, and boxing me in with a hand on either side of my hips.

"Grab the first-aid kit." He calls over his shoulder, and Cooper disappears down the hall without a second thought.

"Now, why the sudden urge to clean?" He raises a brow, staring me down and not giving me an inch to move from where he placed me.

My attention is torn between him in my face and the unshakable need to finish what I set out to do. The fact that the task is left unfinished frustrates me to no end.

"I don't know, because I need to. Now let me down." Trying to slide past him proves to be pointless as he simply puts his hands on my hips, halting me before I can move an inch. Now I can add heat blooming in my core to the list of things overstimulating me.

The newfound heat steals my attention away from the skin-crawling sensation, letting me breathe a little easier for now. But it also zeros in all my focus on the feel of his hands on me and the way he envelops my entire waist without even trying.

"You're not moving, and you're done cleaning." He says like his word is law, sparking that lingering irritation.

Cooper strolls back into the kitchen, any arguments I had halting on the tip of my tongue. He lays the first-aid kit on the counter beside us, opening it up and pulling out various items.

Maverick steps back, pulling my foot up with one hand to look at the bottom of it, poking and prodding until he hits a sensitive spot, making me wince.

He grabs the tweezers from the kit, focusing on grabbing a piece of the mug that's embedded in my heel while Cooper unwraps some antiseptic wipes and bandages.

Maverick is quick to get the mug out of my foot and cleans it up, sealing it off with what I would say is overkill of gauze and tape, wrapping it all the way around my foot rather than just slapping a band-aid on.

Closing up the kit, he points a finger at me.

"Stay." Turning around, he dismisses me quickly, grabbing the broom while Cooper takes the trash bag from the floor, heading to the garage.

"I'm not a dog." I point out, sliding to the edge of the counter.

He drops the broom, grabs my hips, and pushes me back.

"Oh, I know, a dog follows commands much better than you can." He mutters.

"You're such a dick!" I shove at his hands with my one good one, making no progress in getting him out of my way.

He snorts, shaking his head, pissing me off even more.

"What's so funny?"

"Nothing, just that's the first time you've called me that while being in your right mind. Last time you were frying your brain with a fever and insisting you didn't need my help."

He's referring to when I was sick, and he kidnapped me from my dorm. I still don't fully remember, but apparently calling him a dick is my default, whether I realize I'm doing it or not.

"Just let me go so I can clean up the mess."

"Why?" He doesn't budge, and it's so damn irritating.

"Because I made the mess, just let me clean it up."

"No, we all made the mess. So sit your ass still and stop fighting me."

"But I need to!" My anger is back full force, blood running like fire through me once again, burning me up from the inside. He's not getting the need for me to do this; instead, he's insistent on pushing me around and making this so much harder than it needs to be.

"Why do you need to?" He presses.

"Because all I am is a burden! Ever since you brought me here, everyone is doing everything for me, and I do nothing. Then today, I had a chance to clean up, and I needed to because looking at everything lying around was like fire burning all over my body, and the only way to make it stop was to just fix it. But I have this damn sling on, and I can't do anything, then I broke the damn mug and made it worse, and you won't let me fix it. I'm tired of being a problem for everyone. I just want to be normal!" Like a dam breaking, the words just spill out of me, no way to stop them, and no way to filter what I'm saying until it's too late.

I could hear a pin drop in the kitchen. Maverick stares at me in complete shock, Cooper hovers in the doorway just behind him, looking equally as stunned.

My chest heaves with my breath, but admittedly, it feels lighter having said everything that's been bouncing around in my head for the last hour. Realistically, it's been in my mind for much longer than that, but it's only become pressing today.

"Charlotte," Cooper steps forward, slowly, like he's approaching a scared animal. "You are not a burden to any of us."

His words fall on deaf ears, now that the dams been broken, my mind is determined to get it all out before I can catch up.

You all had to take me in, like a fucking stray dog, because I have nowhere else to go. You all heard what my parents think of me, which I'm sure made you feel even more sorry for me. *You* have to help me shower every day because I can't use my arm." I spit at Maverick, as if it's his fault. I know it's not, but I'm on a roll. "Kai and Eli look at me like I'll shatter if they say the wrong thing. You all just decided I could be left alone less than a week ago. Which I'm sure will change now that you've come home to see me having a mental breakdown because there are dishes in the kitchen and blankets on the couch! I'm a mess, admit it or don't, it doesn't make it any less true.

Maverick's nostrils flare, and his face sports a dark, thunderous expression. Cooper, on the other hand, just looks hurt. I instantly regret not keeping my mouth shut and swallowing down my thoughts.

"Charlotte, you can't help any of that. You were attacked, that's not your fault. That left you hurt and unable to do some things; again, that's not your fault, and it's not permanent." He ticks off his fingers with each point. "Kai and Eli were shaken up by everything, but they don't think you're broken or fragile; they just need a chance to recoup. And how you're feeling today is not because you're messed up in any way. Your doctor said that things could be intensified for you while your body tries to regulate itself from coming off the meds your *parents* had you on."

Stepping between Maverick and me, he pushes stray hair that has fallen in my face, tucking it behind my ear and cupping my jaw.

We heard what your parents said, and it's bullshit. We don't feel sorry for you, Charlotte. We care about you more than you realize, and we're not going to run away scared just because you have a bad day. You can have a bad day and feel overwhelmed, but don't call yourself a burden.

All the fight leaves me; I deflate, sinking into Cooper, my head resting on his chest, tears stinging my eyes as a few escape.

I'm used to being written off and discarded as the problem child. I've never had the luxury of someone trying to understand me.

I know they've told me before that they care about me, but hearing it doesn't automatically mean I believe it.

The sincerity in Cooper's voice and his ability to defend each of my points make me believe what he's saying is true. Even if I can't wrap my head around it completely just yet.

I'm just exhausted from constantly feeling at war with myself, always arguing and second-guessing whether what I'm doing is the 'normal' thing to do.

Trying to be normal is exhausting. I don't know if I can do it anymore.

But if what Cooper is saying truly reflects their feelings, then I might not need to try anymore.

13

~ Cooper ~

Seeing Charlotte break down in the kitchen broke my heart. I can't stand to hear her call herself a burden and put herself down because of things that are out of her control.

It's been a couple of days since, and she's remained pretty quiet.

Maverick and I both agreed to go back to work the next day, as if nothing was different, so we didn't make her think that we thought any differently of her.

The twins had been upset when they came home to see her crying against my chest, with the kitchen a mess and not many answers to their endless questions.

I had escaped with Charlotte, taking her up to bed, leaving Mav to answer their questions. And that meant their questions were left unanswered.

It feels like all of our disagreements go unanswered lately, but none of us wants to push her too far and upset her even more, especially not after hearing what she thinks about herself.

Her tears soak through my shirt, and her body falls limply against mine.

Mav looks at me with a horrified expression, never one to be comfortable with tears, and I'm not well practiced with them either.

He took the lead in pushing her over the edge to get her to admit everything she's been bottling up inside, so it seems I'll have to take the lead here.

Per usual, the twins have impeccable timing, waltzing in the front door with dinner in hand, coming to a standstill in the kitchen entry, taking in the scene.

Kai's face darkens seeing Charlotte crying against my chest. Dropping the food on the counter, he's instantly on the defensive.

"What the fuck did you two do to her?" He snarls.

"Why do you automatically assume that we did something?" Mav fires back, blocking his path to where I stand with her.

"Because I've never seen Lottie cry, but coming home from work, here she is in tears and with no one but the two of you around."

"If I recall correctly, it was you two that sent her into a panic attack when she first started working with us." Always with the low blows, Mav.

Kai's left with his mouth gaping open like a fish, and before he can retaliate, I decide to intervene.

"Knock it off, Charlotte's just a bit overstimulated. I'm going to take her up to bed. You guys clean this up and eat your dinner. I'll make sure she's okay." Being mindful of her arm, I slide her off the counter, picking her up in a bridal carry, stepping around the three of them to head to her room.

Kai tries to say something as we pass, but she buries her face further into my chest, hiding from all of us.

His face falls, and he steps back, letting me pass. Eli stands silently where he stopped, looking torn but not interfering.

Stepping into her room, I shut the door with my foot, lying her on her bed and adjusting the blankets around her as she curls up on her side as best she can.

Tears still trail down her face, slowing now but still evident.

Once the blankets are settled, I lie beside her, facing her on my side and helping to prop up her arm with the stuffed dinosaur I got her, making sure she's as comfortable as possible.

I reach out to stroke her hair while she sniffles quietly.

"I'm s-s-sorry." She mumbles, a pink blush spreading over both her cheeks.

"It's okay, just relax."

"I d-don't want to be a p-problem."

She's more thick-headed than Mav, I swear. After everything I just said downstairs, she's still worried about us thinking she's a hassle.

"And you're not." I assure her, "You've been through a lot of shit lately, and it's understandable that you're going to have some bad days. Your doctor said that the meds you were on and are now coming off of could cause an increase in irritation, OCD tendencies, and anxiety. That's all this is: your body is just working to straighten itself out. That's nothing to be sorry for."

She closes her eyes, and for a moment, I think she may have fallen asleep.

"If I w-were just normal, this wouldn't be an issue." She whispers.

"What even is normal?" I fire back, tired of this preconceived notion that she's different from the rest of us. "You had parents who, in my opinion, were pretty shitty, trying to change you your entire life. You went through something pretty traumatic, and your life has been flipped upside down in a matter of a couple of weeks. Nothing about this is normal, and I think that the way you're handling it is exceptional."

"You're just saying that." She sighs, trying to roll away from me, but I cup her jaw with my hand, keeping her from moving away.

"I'm not, Charlotte. I don't say shit to just say it. And I don't waste my time either, so if I'm here with you, it's

because I want to be, and I know the same goes for my brothers too."

She huffs a small laugh, "Maybe for t-three of you that's true."

It seems Mav still hasn't had the talk that he needs to with her. In her eyes, he still wants nothing to do with her, which could be where some of her misguided feelings of being a burden are still festering.

"You'd be surprised," I answer cryptically, knowing it's not my place to have that talk for him.

Her brows pull together, a frown forming on her face as she tries to piece it together.

"Maverick barely tolerates me," She shakes her head. "He just pushes me over the edge and makes me say things I don't want to say."

"Maybe, or maybe he sees that you're holding everything in and he knows firsthand how difficult that is."

Her eyes flicker between mine, looking for the hidden message.

"What a-are you saying?"

"It doesn't matter," I deflect. "Maybe you need to talk to someone, though. Have you given any thought to what your doctor said? About seeing someone to talk and get an updated diagnosis?"

I can feel her heart beat speed up under my hand and her eyes drop to stare at my chest.

She shakes her head.

"Look, we won't force you to do anything, but I think it could be helpful for you."

She doesn't respond, and it's clear she won't. This has been a sensitive subject since we've met, and I don't think it'll get any easier anytime soon.

I lean forward, kissing her forehead, silently dropping it for now.

I try to pull away to leave her to rest, but her hand shoots out, grabbing my shirt.

"Please, s-stay." Her voice is so small and childlike that I have no way to say no.

Settling in, I let her shuffle forward, tentatively laying her head on my arm. Within minutes, she's out.

A knock on the door startles me, pulling me out of my head.

"Come in," I call to the other side of the door. It opens a moment later, Mav strolling into my office with a hard expression, tossing a manila folder on my desk.

"What's up?" I ask, watching as he drops down into one of the chairs, nodding to the folder.

"We just got another case, a missing person."

Flipping through the file, I see the general information, person description, and the contact information for the family that hired us.

"Okay, we get these all the time. Why is this one making you look like someone pissed in your cornflakes this morning?"

"Look where she went missing." He demands.

Confused, I flip through the file again, reading the family's comments, and instantly, my blood runs cold.

The Tilted Kilt.

"She was taken from the same bar as Ivy?"

"Yup." Mav nods, looking like he chewed on something sour. "Close to the same age, same bar, and no trail for the cops to follow."

"We already turned over the case for Ivy, though. Why don't they just follow the lead that Charlotte found to see if it's a match to her case?"

He leans forward, running his hands through his hair, dragging them down his face.

"I just got off a call with the sheriff. They tried to trace the lead she found, and the trail went cold. With nothing more prominent for them to look into, they tossed the case back. He said they're swamped and don't have the capacity to spend any more of their resources digging into a cold case."

I think back to the blow-up between him and Mav when he banned her from pursuing the case any further. I can't imagine he's just going to let her jump back into it because we have a matching victim.

"So, what? You want to take it back over and work it? After all the shit you went through with Charlotte?"

"I don't know!" He jumps up, pacing the room. "He said they were going to write off the cases if we didn't take them over."

I narrow my eyes at him.

"But you don't want to do that." I observe, "Because you know that she can find more if you let her."

Heaving a sigh, he stops, gripping the back of the chair and staring me down.

"Yes," He spits out. And I can see it pains him to admit it. "I can't sit here and let them write it off when I know we have Charlotte. I know she can find more, I just don't want to put her at risk like that. We still don't even know who attacked her."

He's right. Charlotte digging further into this case will put a target on her back if the wrong people find out. But we're also not the type to give up on the cases that the cops can't solve. It's the whole reason we opened GLS in the first place.

"You said you had someone working on her attack? Someone outside of the office?" I confirm.

He nods.

"Okay, then we let her work this." He goes to argue, but I hold up a hand, stopping him. "We let her work it, but we work it with her. Don't let her do any of it alone; she has to check in with everything that she finds, and if it comes to finding where either of the girls is, then she stays far away from it."

"And you think she'll just follow those rules blindly?" He has his doubts, and I get it; she's proven to be more stubborn than any of us combined.

"I think you'd be surprised what she'll agree to if it means that she can do what she loves to do."

14

~ Charlotte ~

I hate hospitals. I think that's officially decided by now.

But today, it's not too bad, because I'm walking out finally without the hindrance of the sling that I've been stuck in since waking up.

I can't wait to go home and use a computer with two fully functional arms and hands.

It's a good day, and I'm trying to keep that positive attitude, despite the doctor's attempts to set me up with a private consultation yet again to discuss my inaccurate diagnosis.

Personally, I don't want to deal with it. I've believed one thing about myself for years: talking with a doctor for an hour isn't going to change how I feel about myself. I guess that's what having parents who can't stand your existence will do to you.

I haven't heard from them once since I woke up to find them in my hospital room, and I'm not sure I want to after seeing how easy it was for them to discard me and walk away.

"So, what are we going to do to celebrate now that you have two arms again?" Kai skips beside me, holding open the door with a flourish, gesturing for me to go first.

"I'd like to go use a computer to my full ability. That sounds like fun."

Soaking in the sunshine, I ignore his pouting.

"That's so lame! You're going to have plenty of time to do that when you go back to work on Monday. We need to do something fun or adventurous."

"She still has to take it easy and rehab her arm," Eli points out from my other side. "Not sure how adventurous she can be just yet."

"Okay, but we still have to do something more exciting than going home to play on the computer. We can do that any day."

Getting in the car, I take the passenger seat, Kai in the driver's seat, and Eli in the back. Buckling up, I turn to face him.

"What did you have in mind?" I concede. As much as I want to go home and dive into Ivy's case, I wouldn't get any work done with him hovering around. Besides, I was already frustrated this morning when my video files got corrupted yet again. I'm still at a dead end, and it's driving me insane. Between that and the doctor's appointment, I could use a mental break.

"Yes!" He pumps his fist, smiling widely. "Well, we could go to Myth, they're having a decades theme night tonight."

Scrunching my nose up, I shake my head. Remembering the loud and overwhelming atmosphere from last time. Not exactly the mental break I'm looking for.

"Okayyy, we could go bowling?" He suggests.

Eli laughs, "With a freshly healed broken collar bone?"

"Good point." Kai nods, "No bowling. Oh! What about the drive-in?"

"That's all the way out in Lake City," Eli argues.

"So, it's not a bad drive, and we'll get there just in time for the first showing."

My interest is piqued. I've seen drive-in movies in TV shows growing up, but I've never been. It sounds more appealing than a normal movie, crammed into a row with a bunch of strangers who just talk or chew on obnoxious snacks the whole time.

"What's playing?" I ask.

Kai pulls out his phone, typing away, laughing when he sees the movie listed.

"Twilight."

Tilting my head, I ask, "The vampire movie?"

"Yep." Eli groans in the backseat.

"Oh come on, it's the drive-in, a crappy movie is part of the experience. It'll be fun."

It sounds like fun, but Eli sounds like he'd rather chew on glass than go. Looking into the backseat, I raise a brow, wondering if he'd be mad if I said I want to go.

He studies my face for a moment, rolling his eyes before giving in.

"Fine, we'll go. But we need to stop by the house to change and grab blankets and shit so we're at least comfortable while we suffer."

With another cheer, Kai starts up the car, heading back towards the house.

Another hour later, and we're pulling up to the drive-in in the middle of nowhere on what looks like someone's family farm.

Hand-painted signs are set up to direct people where to go.

Kai pays the cash fee to get in, and we find a parking spot in the middle of the bunch.

A makeshift screen stands before all the cars, playing movie trailers for films that came out years ago.

A snack tent is set up off to the left of the cars, and bathrooms are set up to the right.

The cars are evenly spaced in the field, leaving plenty of space for those who opted to bring chairs and set up outside their cars.

Kai made sure to back into our spot, and he jumps out to pop the tailgate, moving the pillows and blankets around that we brought.

The sun is just beginning to set, casting a breathtaking orange and pink hue across the whole sky.

"I'll go grab the snacks," Eli tells us, jumping out of the back and towards the snack tent.

"Don't forget my cherry slushie!" Kai calls out, laughing at the finger Eli tosses over his shoulder.

Climbing out of the car, I round to the back to see Kai's setup.

He's laid the back seats down, spreading out comforters and propping the pillows behind the front seats to give us a full bed's worth of space.

Smiling at me, he nods towards the space.

"Hop in, I'm going to get the sound set up.

Feeling excited by his eager energy, I kick off my shoes and climb in.

When we went home for supplies, we all changed into comfortable clothes. I opted for a pair of baggy sweatpants and a well-worn band tee.

They were both dressed similarly in plain shirts and gray sweatpants, which made me understand what the girls in the romance novels I've read were talking about. An unfamiliar flutter kicked up in my stomach, seeing the way they both looked, filling out the offensive material.

The comforters that Kai laid out give a good cushion to the hard floor, making it extremely comfortable to lie on. And the open tailgate gives us a perfect view of the movie screen.

Within seconds, the car radio comes to life, filling the car with the audio of the movie trailers playing before us.

He jumps into the back, sliding into place beside me and shifting around until he's comfortable.

He catches me watching him, shooting me a wink while he tosses a hand behind his head.

"What do you think, Lottie-girl?"

"It's pretty cool, way better than a movie theater."

"That's the spirit." He agrees, just as Eli approaches with snacks. "Ah, and our own personal snack waiter."

Balancing a tray of snacks and drinks, he manages to throw a bag of candy at Kai's head, which he narrowly catches.

"Real funny, asshole, you get to go for refills."

He sets the tray down in the bed, an arrangement of popcorn, nachos, sour candy, and drinks laid out for us before climbing in on my other side.

Heat instantly engulfs me, pressed between both of them. It makes me tense to have no space between them, but strangely, it's also comforting.

They both dig into the snacks, dead set on devouring them before the trailers even end. I pick through the popcorn, loving the salty flavor and the way it pairs with the blue slushie Eli offered me.

The movie starts, and a hush falls over the car, all of us focused on the screen. I know I've seen the film before, back when it came out, but I've never been a big movie watcher, so I don't remember much of it.

All of the snacks are gone before we reach the halfway point of the film, and the three of us are sprawled out with the trash discarded at the foot of the bed.

I've been trying to focus on the movie for the last twenty minutes, but I've been distracted, watching Kai inch his hand closer and closer to my thigh.

He's subtle, shifting closer every few minutes, never moving too fast to completely steal my attention. But I still notice.

Feeling brave, or stupid, and unable to ignore the heat flaming inside me, I shift closer to him so his hand reaches its target.

His hand envelops my thigh, the heat from his touch seeping through my sweats and setting me on fire.

My heart thumps widely in my chest while I wait for his next move.

He doesn't leave me waiting; his other hand comes from behind his head to catch my jaw, turning my face towards his.

His eyes meet mine, looking to my lips and back before he leans in, giving me plenty of time to pull away before his lips land on mine.

Sparks bloom instantly, shooting off like fireworks behind my eyes while our breaths mingle together.

The movie is forgotten, the sound is no longer heard, and everything goes silent. The only thing I know is him and me, and I don't have to think; I just follow his lead. His tongue brushes mine, pulling back quickly while I chase it, wanting more of the cherry slush flavor.

A small moan pries its way past my lips seconds before he pulls back, leaving me panting. I try to chase his lips, but his hand holds me back. Another hand catches my jaw, turning me towards Eli, and Kai's hand tightens on my thigh, encouraging me.

I dive right in, wanting more now that I've had a taste, feeling the differences between their kisses. Eli is more dominant in the way his lips devour mine, whereas Kai is gentle and teasing.

Eli's hand slides down to cup the back of my neck, kneading it lightly as his tongue wars with mine, dissolving any lingering tension as I melt fully into him.

Kai's hand continues to explore, moving up from my thigh, stopping to squeeze my waist, adding to the sensations rushing through me from both their hands.

Eli tears his lips from mine, his head ducking down to my neck, hitting another spot that makes me see stars while Kai's hand travels upwards.

I'm gasping for air at the feel of Eli's lips biting and sucking my neck, his hands find my hips, turning me towards him, while Kai's other hand comes around my waist, trapping me from both sides.

Instinctively, I throw a leg over Eli's hips, my own shooting forward, searching for something I can't explain.

Eli comes back to steal another kiss, my breath leaving my lungs when I feel Kai's hands slip under my shirt, continuing their trek upwards.

His hands settle over both my breasts, and shockwaves rattle me when he squeezes them both.

Eli pulls back, his eyes searching while I gasp for air.

"You okay?" He asks breathlessly.

Taking stock of my body, I'm overwhelmed, feeling too many things to distinguish one from the other. But more than that, I'm desperate for more, for my mind to be so preoccupied with everything to truly feel just one thing.

Nodding frantically, I pray that they'll keep going.

Hearing my silent plea, he nods to Kai over my shoulder, they both move in unison. Kai's hands capture the hem of my t-shirt, sliding it up to expose my bra, resting it under my chin. His hands move down to catch my hips, pulling me back into him, and his lips land on the side of my neck, opposite of where Eli's were moments ago.

My eyes fall shut, savoring the feel of his lips on me, my head falls to the side, giving him more room to explore.

My eyes fly open again when I feel Eli's lips land on my sternum, his tongue trailing down between my breasts.

For a split second, I cringe at the wet feeling it leaves behind, but I quickly yell at that part of my brain to shut the hell up, drowning in the heat that's swallowing me whole.

Sounds I've never heard escape me when Kai's teeth graze my skin. Something about that spot must be hardwired to my core, his teeth on my skin making my hips rock yet again.

I feel the cup of my bra being pulled to the side, and I drop my head to watch Eli's tongue as it circles around my breast, hitting every nerve ending possible except where I need him most.

Before I can embarrass myself by begging, his lips seal around my nipple, biting and sucking and sending me into another dimension.

My head spins, I think I'm on the verge of blacking out. Suffocating in my own pleasure, I can only faintly hear the moans spilling from my lips before Kai pulls my head towards him, silencing me with his lips on mine. He's like a lifeline, offering me air when I can't capture my own, keeping me afloat to ride the wave I landed on.

Eli moves to the other breast, starting over and driving me higher when his fingers find the first.

My hips buck frantically, blindly searching until they brush against his thigh, bringing a delicious friction that I can't ignore.

With each pass, I'm taken higher and higher, getting more desperate until I think I'm having a seizure with how my body is convulsing.

I don't know what I'm rushing towards, but in unison, Eli's teeth bite down on my breast, and Kai's settle into that spot on my neck again.

My vision goes white, and a kaleidoscope of colors bursts, moving in every direction, blinding me.

I go completely stiff, trying to hold on to this feeling forever, but just like the wave that brought it on, it brings me down slowly, peaking in small bursts before fading away.

When my vision clears, my chest is heaving, I feel like I've run a marathon, and my body is falling limp.

Eli pulls my bra back into place, sliding my shirt back down and brushing a kiss on my forehead. Kai soothes the spot on my neck, still pulsing from his bite.

Neither of them says a word. Eli shifts to lie back down on my side, and Kai settles behind me, his arm around my waist, keeping me tucked into him. My head lands on Eli's chest, unable to hold itself up any longer as exhaustion overtakes me.

I don’t have a chance to ask them about what just happened before I start to slip away, falling asleep to the sounds of Edward coming to rescue Bella.

15

~ Kai ~

I've always loved the drive-in. This weekend only further proved that point, our fun movie night turned into a spicy encounter.

I've never felt closer to Lottie than in the back of my car that night.

I half expected her to freak out after, maybe regret hooking up in the back of the car, but the rest of the weekend was surprisingly chill. She and Eli holed up in her room, looking at their computer nerd stuff all day, then the three of us met Mav and Coop for dinner at one of our favorite diners. Yesterday we were all home, and with an unexpected storm that rolled through, it became another movie day, minus the heavy make-out session, much to my displeasure.

She seemed lighter after our night together, either from the night that we had, the sling being gone, or just having passed from the bad day she'd had a couple of nights before when we'd come home to find her crying in the kitchen. It could also be that she's going back to work today, and unlike anyone else I know, she's really excited about that.

Either way, it's nice to see her in such good spirits. My only hope is that work doesn't ruin her mood. Mav tends to be overly demanding and tough at the office, which could easily sour her mood.

The bright side is that since we had to drop that Ivy girl's case, things have been much easier to manage. A lot of low-profile cases with simple solutions, and plenty of wins. I think a win would do Lottie good, especially after losing that case she cared so much about.

She's taking her online classes, so I don't get to see her for most of the day; all of mine are currently on campus.

The second my last lecture lets out, I'm flying out the doors, racing to my car with one thing on my mind: seeing my girl.

You would think that living under the same roof would alleviate some of my infatuation with her, but it hasn't, not in the slightest. I'm still just as obsessed with her as I was the first day I laid eyes on her.

Pulling up to GLS in record time, I remind myself not to rush in there acting like a caveman. Coop was supposed to pick up Lottie and bring her to work so she wouldn't be walking alone, and that's what I need to trust happened. I cannot dictate how she lives her life, and I came off looking like an asshole the last time I made a fuss about her choosing what she wanted to do.

Walking in the front, I actively ignore Sascha's presence behind the desk, still a bit pissed that she still works here after some of the comments she's thrown Lottie's way. I'm sure she's said much worse to her when we weren't around, but Coop could never get her to admit it.

When Mav was stressed in the hospital, with his phone blowing up from Sascha's ridiculous, flirty text messages, he threatened to fire her for her inappropriate behavior, but she broke down in crocodile tears, claiming she was jealous and stressed. He cut her some slack, but I hope she shows her true colors and she's out on her ass sooner rather than later.

Mav's office is empty as I pass by, Coop's door is shut, so I can't tell what he's up to. Dropping my bag off on my desk, I see Eli's office is empty, meaning he must have had a later lecture than I did today.

More alone time with my Lottie-girl.

A quick knock on her door and I let myself in, freezing when I find Mav sitting on the opposite side of her desk, folders laid out between them.

"Uh, hey. Sorry, I didn't know you were in here." I tell Mav, nodding to Lottie.

He sits back in his chair, crossing his arms with a rare, amused expression covering his features.

"That's the thing about knocking, typically you wait for a response before barging in." He muses.

I have to double-take; I'm not used to him cracking jokes.

"What if we were indecent?"

I nearly choke on my own spit, completely caught off guard. Lottie, red as a tomato, starts sputtering.

"W-we weren't *indecent.* W-we were just t-talking."

"He knows that," Mav says, standing, leaving the files behind, and stepping around me. "Let me know when you read over those, and if you need any help with anything, just shout."

Her cheeks remain flushed as she stares down at her desk, clearly embarrassed. It's funny to think that after what we did the other night, she's still embarrassed by such a playful comment.

"So, what were you two *talking* about?" Wiggling my eyebrows, I kick my feet up on the desk, making myself at home.

"I got a new case." A smile pulls at her lips, unable to be contained.

"Oh yeah?"

She nods, stopping quickly as her brows crinkle.

"Or I guess an old case, technically. That Ivy Gilbert case that I started on, I'm picking that back up."

"I thought Maverick was against you working that after you found a dark web listing?" I recall the events that led to her not speaking to him for over a week.

"Right, but apparently JSO threw it back at Maverick; he didn't want to abandon it, so he's letting me work it again."

"Just like that? He threw that whole fit to just waltz back in here and had you the files as if nothing happened?"

She tilts her head side to side. "Technically, he has rules in place that he 'expects me to follow,' but yeah, pretty much." Her air-quoting Maverick is the greatest thing I've seen today. It's clear that she has no intention of following whatever ridiculous rules he's laid out.

"What's the new file?" I ask, seeing two different folders on the desk.

Grabbing it, she flips it open, eager to show it off.

"Another missing person, but it matches Ivy's case."

"How do they match?" I pull the file towards me to take a closer look.

She starts tapping away on her keyboard, pulling something up on her monitors.

"Same age, same details regarding their disappearance, and same bar."

"Same bar?"

She nods, confirming.

What are the odds that another girl goes missing from the same bar Ivy was taken from? I'm not one to believe in coincidences, so I'd say it's definitely suspicious.

"Well, at least it's a case that you already have a lot built up on. Didn't you find a whole listing for sale of Ivy before Mav freaked?"

"Yeah, and I've managed to get a list of names who viewed the link, and I'm working on separating names who sent inquiries on it so we can start digging into those to see who might have her." Briefly, I wonder how she got that far back into the case when Mav just gave it back to her, but Eli walking in interrupts my thought process.

"My lecture ran late," He shoves my feet off the desk, dropping into the chair next to mine. "What'd I miss?"

"Lottie was just telling me about Mav giving her Ivy's case back, along with a duplicate."

His eyes narrow, looking skeptically at me, then Lottie.

"Is that so?"

She nods, still typing away, but she turns the screen to face us suddenly.

"I'm still trying to get the software to work to ID him, but I pulled the video footage from the night Ivy went missing, and the night Valarie went missing, and look." Pointing at the screen, I see two images side by side. Both are grainy, but it's clear that it's security footage from the Tilted Kilt.

I can make out Ivy in the image on the left, remembering seeing pictures of her from her case file and from when we went to Georgia to interview her parents. On the right is another girl, a small redhead, looking to be around Ivy's age.

"It's the same guy," Eli observes, and when I take another look, I see he's right. Both images have different girls, but each shows the same man ushering them through the crowded bar.

"The same guy that I can't get an ID on, but yeah." Lottie pouts, pulling the screen back towards her to continue working.

"Have you tried any other software? Or is that the same program as before?"

"Both, I tried the original program that I had, but the last few weeks I've been testing different ones. All of them come out corrupted."

A lot of their tech talk goes over my head, but I manage to catch on to the fact that she just mentioned working on this for weeks, and my dear old twin didn't even bat an eye.

"What about the list that you had? Can you ID from that and then cross-match it with the footage?"

"I could try, but the IDs take a while to pull all the accurate information; it's going to be tedious to pick through that list and try to compare."

"You dirty little traitors!" I finally blurt out when I've had enough of the nerd talk.

Lottie's wide eyes stare back at me, and Eli just tosses a bored expression my way.

"What are you talking about?" He asks dryly.

"You two never gave up on this case; you've been working on it for weeks! Is this why you keep blowing me off with Dragonlight? So you two can work on this?" I ask Lottie, her guilty expression is enough of an answer. "Unbelievable."

I'm half-pretending to be this hurt; I am a little pissed, though, that they kept this from me. They didn't even ask for my help. Sure, I'm not a tech guru, but I can be useful in other ways.

"It w-wasn't like that." Lottie placates me, "I wasn't supposed to be working on any of it, and Eli didn't know until like two weeks ago because I needed to go get my hard drive." She looks guilty, spitting out explanations as if I'm truly mad at her.

"It's fine, I just don't like being left out." Pouting, I try to earn more of her sympathy.

"You don't know anything about computers other than how to play video games. Why would she come to you for help hacking into a security system?" Eli retorts, "Not to mention, she was doing this in secret, and you have a big mouth."

"I do not!"

"You kind of do," Lottie agrees, ramping up my offense to their claims. "Which isn't a bad thing, I just really needed to keep this quiet," She tries to amend.

"Whatever, the point is now that you're back on the case, I want to help, however you'll let me."

Lottie nods, quick to agree. Eli tilts his head, drumming his fingers across the desk, contemplating.

"How about another trip to Georgia?" He asks cryptically, and I have a feeling I'm not going to like this.

16

~ Maverick ~

I hate that we have to sit by while Charlotte digs around for more information about the missing girls, but the thought of tossing the cases when there was a chance we could find them made my stomach turn.

It's only been a couple of days since I gave her the cases, and she's hit the ground running.

I had planned to ease her back into work, not wanting to put too much on her too fast, but it would seem life had other plans.

Cooper and I both made it clear when she started working on these that there needed to be boundaries so she wouldn't dig herself into a hole or run herself into the ground. From what I could tell, so far, she was abiding by that.

It's a Friday afternoon, and I'm wrapping up for the day, ready to have a weekend off to take a break. It's been hectic around here since Charlotte was in the hospital; there are a lot of loose ends from last year that need to be tied up.

I was also anxious to get out of here because, for one of the first times, I'd have some time to spend with Charlotte without the twins hovering off to the side. She sent the twins back up to Georgia to question our new missing person's parents and also to go check out the bar in person that both had disappeared from. I know the two of them could fend for themselves, but I was just glad that she didn't try to insist on going herself.

Cooper offered to make himself scarce, but I'm not afraid to admit that I want him around to act as a buffer, or to keep me from saying the wrong thing and fucking all of this up.

I've been wanting to talk to her about my feelings for her, but no time has felt right. Even now, it doesn't seem like a good time, but with the twins gone, it was the best opportunity I was going to get.

A soft knock sounds at my door, bringing me back to reality. Calling for them to come in, Charlotte's head peeks around the door, glancing at the room for stepping in to take a seat.

She looks tired, not exhausted and drained like I've seen her before, but just like it's been a long day full of dead ends for her.

"Done for today?" I ask, starting to close out the tabs that I've been working on for the past few hours.

"Yeah, I can't stare at any more identification reports while trying to cross-match strangers on a never-ending list."

"Sounds boring." I can't even pretend that sounds interesting at this point.

I see her nod out of the corner of my eye, slumping back in the chair to rub her eyes under her glasses, fixing her hair in a messy bun atop her head.

"So nothing new with any of that then?" I ask just to make small talk while I gather my things and lead her out of the office, locking up behind us.

"Not really, unless you count the discovery of hidden underground subway tunnels underneath Jax's downtown that I found out about."

"How'd that come up?" I faintly remember hearing about hidden tunnels in the city back when I was in school, but the public wasn't allowed down there, and they're said to have been abandoned in the seventies.

"One of the names on the list owned one of the buildings said to be over a tunnel's entrance." I open the car door for her, helping her step in. "I kind of went down a rabbit hole when I noticed it." She adds when I hop in beside her.

It's interesting for sure, but nothing that will help us find the girls, unfortunately.

"Cooper should be home soon. Anything you want to get for dinner?"I don't know why I feel so awkward, like a high schooler on their first date. It's even more awkward when I remind myself that Charlotte doesn't reciprocate those feelings, simply because I've been an emotionless dick around her for the most part.

That's my own fault, now I'm left floundering, wondering how to tell her that I actually do see her as something more, and I care for her the way that my brothers do, not just in a protective older brother way.

"Whatever the two of you want, I'm sure it will be fine."

"Charlotte," I'm ready to just blurt it out so that we can move forward. Either she'll be open to it, or she'll rightfully tell me to fuck off. Either way, I can't take this tension I've built up in my head.

I see her looking at me while I keep my eyes on the windscreen.

"I wanted to talk to you about something-"My phone blaring through the sound system cuts me off. Biting back a curse, I slam the answer button, already annoyed with whoever's on the other end. "What?" I bark out.

Crowd noise fills the car, and Cooper's voice yells to be heard above it.

"Did you and Charlotte eat yet?" I watch her wince from his yelling.

"No, we were going to wait for you to get home."

"Well, don't! Come to Joe's, they're having trivia night, two-dollar beers, and I need a team!" He sounds like he's already had a beer or two. Coop has always had an obsession with trivia, either playing trivia games or learning pointless facts to spout at any given moment. I can't remember the last time he dragged any of us to a trivia night; they honestly don't pop up often, since it's not a very popular activity among most people here.

I look over at Charlotte, raising a brow and asking if she'd be cool with going out.

She fights a smile, her shoulders shaking with withheld laughter, and she shrugs her shoulders, leaving it up to me.

"We'll be there in ten," I tell him, swiftly ending the call.

"What's Joe's?" She questions once the line is clear.

Leveling a stare at her, I wait for her reaction, "Seafood bar."

Instantly, her nose scrunches up, her face clearly labeling her disgust.

That's what I figured. I've only ever seen her eat chicken, and occasionally a cheeseburger; something told me she wasn't a closet seafood connoisseur.

"They have some plain food too, don't look so worried," I assure her, mockingly.

"I wasn't worried." She mutters, looking out the window.

"Right, you weren't just panicking about having to tear apart cute little crabs or shrimp so you can toss away their carcass and gorge on their bodies while worrying about if they were boiled alive or not." I can help but poke fun at her. I don't know why she doesn't like seafood; just that her face made it clear she doesn't, so tossing out the most morbid explanation as to why wasn't necessary, but seeing her flaming face reaction is too good to pass up.

"Well, I am now." She stares at me, horrified, with wide eyes and a chill racking her frame.

"Relax, I'll protect you from any shellfish." Pulling into the bar, I hop out, opening her door for her.

"Sure you will." She mutters, following behind me, and I'm glad because it means she can't see the smile I can't wipe off my face.

The bar is loud from the second I open the door. Rather than walking ahead of me, she huddles into my side, as if I can act as a barrier between her and the noise. She doesn't even flinch when I drop my arm around her to keep her close while I walk us through the crowd.

Thankfully, Cooper had the foresight to grab a booth in the back corner, so it at least gives the semblance of privacy and a buffer from the crowd.

"Hey! You made it!" Cooper stands, wrapping Charlotte up in a hug, pulling her down to sit next to him in the rounded booth, leaving me to close in the other side.

She stiffens for a moment when she finds herself in the middle of the two of us, but composes herself quickly when Cooper pulls her into a conversation about her day.

Coop ordered us all a round of beers that are ready and waiting on the table. I grab mine, downing half of it in one go.

Charlotte takes her glass as Cooper talks her ear off, sniffing the contents before taking a tentative sip. She tries to hide her distaste for it, but I catch it. It doesn't seem that she's a beer drinker.

While they talk, I grab a waitress to put in another round of beers, but I change Charlotte's drink, asking the waitress to bring her something fruit-filled and girly. The night we picked her up from Myth, she'd been wasted on cocktails, so it seems like a safer bet than the beer.

Her eyes light up when the tall glass, filled to the brim with a bubbly strawberry concoction, is set in front of her, eagerly sipping on it while she listens intently to whatever Cooper is rambling about.

The announcer begins calling for the trivia to start, detailing the rules and passing out answer sheets to each assembled team.

"Really?" I roll my eyes when I see the team name Coop filled in for us.

Charlie's Angels.

"It's funny! And it works because her nickname is Charlie." He shrugs, bumping a shoulder with hers, bringing a smile to her face.

God, he's such a lightweight, two or three beers, and he resorts to teenage jokes and flirting.

"How did that nickname even come about?" I ask, never having learned why Eli came up with Charlie when Kai always called her Lottie.

"Chatroom username," She answers plainly, "Eli thought I was a guy." She holds it together for a grand total of three and a half seconds before bursting into laughter. Coop and I quickly follow.

Our laughter fades out as the announcer comes over the mic to begin the game. The drinks keep flowing, and the questions keep coming before I finally realize we may actually have a shot of winning with Charlotte on our team.

The problem with Coop forcing us to play trivia is that he sucks at it, like royally sucks.

He's stopped questioning how she knows any of the crap they're asking, just blindly writing it down.

"What year did the Titanic sink?" The announcer calls the next question.

Finally, one that I know.

"1912." I say, the exact moment that Charlotte spews out her answer.

"1913."

We both stare at one another, neither one of us wanting to admit the other is right.

"Okay," Cooper drawls, "Which is it? 12 or 13?"

"It's 12."

"13." Again, we speak at the same time, refusing to give in.

Coop tosses the pen into the middle of the table, grabbing his beer. "Great, we're going to lose because you two can't make up your minds."

"Look, I know I'm right, so put 1912," I tell him.

"Hey, what if I know I'm right?" She crosses her arms, leaning forward on the table.

I forgot how direct she can be when she's tipsy.

Matching her stance, I lean forward. "What are you willing to bet on it?"

"What do you want?"

She doesn't know it, but she's laid out a golden opportunity for me here. I know I'm right, so I can call the bet for anything I want, and if she agrees to it, then it's mine. How forward do I want to be? Is the question.

"You." I watch her brows shoot up in surprise, her confident stance faltering, and she pulls her hands towards her lap, I'm assuming to fidget with.

"M-me? What do you mean?"

Cooper's watching like he's front row at a tennis match, head swiveling from side to side. We may as well give the fucker some popcorn so he's truly entertained.

"It means, if I win, then I get a date. You and me, *alone*, my choice."

She blinks, "W-why would you w-want that?"

"I have my reasons, now you won't win, but *if* you do, what do you want?" Whatever she counters is pointless, but I'm still curious to see what she asks for.

She still looks confused, but pushes it aside to make her demand.

"I want Zeus to come into the office for a month."

Well, that was not what I was expecting. Zeus can come into the office any day; he has his own bed and bowls there, from when I used to run with him to work every day.

"Zeus can co-" I slap a hand over Cooper's mouth, stopping him mid-sentence.

"It's a deal." I stick my hand out for Charlotte. She eyes it skeptically, stealing glances at my hand over Coop's mouth before placing her hand in mine, sealing the deal.

I should probably feel bad, this is borderline manipulating her into a date with me… but I'm too proud of how this played out that I can't find any guilt in me. She can always back out, and I wouldn't bat an eye; it all comes down to her choice.

We play the rest of the game without any other arguments over answers, snacking on baskets of fries as we go.

When it comes time to read off the correct answers, both Charlotte and I slide to the edge of our seats, waiting to see who is right.

As the list goes on, and Charlotte's tally of right answers stacks up, I start to second-guess my cockiness. But then the announcer gets to the Titanic question, pausing for dramatic effect before finally confirming my victory with the answer of 1912.

She gapes at me in disbelief.

Leaning back, I savor my beer, relishing in my victory. "I'll pick you up tomorrow at eight o'clock." Shooting her a wink, her face flames yet again, a pout tugging at her lips.

"We live together," she rolled her eyes, her arms crossed over her chest. "How did you even know that?"

I can't stop Cooper this time around, "He spent high school using the Titanic for every book report topic. He practically learned about it for four years straight." Snickering, he raises his hand for another round.

In the end, our team managed to take home third place. I managed to leave with a date, a drunk brother, and a tipsy Charlotte.

I dump Cooper in the backseat and help steady Charlotte in the front before heading out.

"I can't believe we got third place! We're so smart." Cooper slurs, holding his trophy up with one hand from where he's lying across the bench seat in the back.

"I think you mean *Charlotte* won third place," I point out, shaking my head. "You just wrote the answers. Besides, we could have had a second if *someone* didn't fight me on when the Titanic sank."

Charlotte's tears her gaze from the window, head swinging to face me, her hair slapping me in the face as she moves.

"That was one question, and I almost got it! We got third because Cooper wrote Sorcerer's hat instead of *sorting* hat for the Harry Potter question."

Her petulance at Coop's mistake is adorable; she's been hanging out with Kai too much and is quick to pout when things don't go her way. He makes sure everything goes her way.

"That's the best I've ever done, and it got you two to agree to a date, so it seems like everybody wins." Cooper's voice begins to trail off, and a quick glance in the mirror tells me he's starting to fall asleep.

"It was just a bet, Maverick doesn't actually want to go on a date. He was just trying to psych me out."

"I don't know…" He sings. "Maverick and Charlie sitting in a tree K-I-SSSSSSSSSSS-ING I-N-G."

"You do realize that she's *your* girlfriend, right?" I point out.

He sits up, brows furrowed, "You're right." His face pops up between mine and Charlotte's seat, "What are you doing kissing my girlfriend, dick?"

We're already pulling into the driveway, so I check the brakes, sending him flying forward into the seats until he's flung back into the backseat.

"Calm down, you won't remember in the morning."

I hop out of the car, watching him mumble under his breath, rounding the car to where Charlotte slides out.

His expression lights up when he sees her.

"My Char! Hey, I have a nickname for you now." He laughs at his own bad joke, and she stands patiently, watching him with an amused grin.

"Whatever you want." Patting him on the chest, she stumbles a step when he swoops down, grabbing her cheeks and planting a kiss on her lips.

It only lasts a couple of seconds, and Cooper is pulling back, blowing her a kiss, and stumbling up the front steps into the house.

"I think he forgot I live here." She laughs, watching him drop his keys at the front door.

"I think it's safe to say it's time to call it a night." I usher her forward, into the house now that Coop managed to get his keys in the door.

"I had f-fun." She admits quietly. She turns to head upstairs, and I catch her hand, stopping her.

"Just so we're clear, I wasn't psyching you out. I'll be looking forward to our date tomorrow." Squeezing her hand once, I let it go.

She doesn't move; she stands staring at me. Heading to my office, I leave her to work it out in her head, however she needs to.

"A deal's a deal." I toss over my shoulder, shutting myself in my office for the rest of the night.

I may have a mental break from work this weekend, but that unfortunately only applies to clerical work. I still need to find out who attacked Charlotte and whether they're going to try again. It was taking longer than I would like for my guy to find anything, and I was starting to get impatient. Anxiety builds up each time she leaves the house, never knowing if that will be the time they strike again.

We've done a good job of keeping by her side, but that will only last so long with her stubbornness.

I just hope I can find something before one of us slips up.

17

~ Charlotte ~

"And he asked you on a date?" Kai's voice comes through my headphones as I walk on the treadmill in the home gym.

"He didn't ask; he made a bet with me, and he won. He picked a date." I just got done giving him and Eli a recap of our trivia night last night. Waking up this morning, I luckily wasn't hungover, but I was confused about where this whole date thing was coming from with Maverick. It was very out of left field for him.

"About time," I hear Eli mutter.

"If he bet you for a date, then he must want to take you out. Go and try to have a good time." Kai's answer seems vague, and I'm not understanding why they're so okay with Maverick taking me out. Last time we all talked about our relationship, it was just Eli, Cooper, and Kai. Maverick wanted no part of that, as far as I understand. In fact, if I recall correctly, he said that he wouldn't want to hook up with 'some kid' when I caught him and Cooper talking about me.

"You don't think it's weird?"

"I think it's weird that it's taken him this long to pull his head out of his ass and man up." Eli chimes in, sounding annoyed.

They genuinely think that Maverick is doing this because he *likes* me. There's no way that's true. *Maverick.* The man who looks at me like an annoying kid sister who's more of a bother than anything else in his daily life. The one who barks at me to eat, or sleep, or drink water, or stop working; that man does not want to date me.

"What do we even talk about? If we aren't talking about work, then we're arguing."

"Just let him take the lead," Kai says.

"Or you could just ask him why he wanted to go on a date in the first place." Eli offers. I hear a slap, and if I had to guess, Kai smacked Eli upside the head. "I'm just saying, don't spend the whole date worrying about it when you can just ask him."

I hate when people say not to worry about something you're clearly worrying about. It's like telling someone with a broken leg to just stop hurting. It doesn't help anything; it just ramps up the irritation I feel with myself for being worried in the first place.

"So did you find anything new?" I swiftly change the subject, done subjecting myself to further embarrassment from my overthinking.

"Nothing yet, we met with Valarie's parents, just confirmed the information they already gave us. We're getting ready now to head to the Tilted Kilt to see if we can find anything there." Eli tells me.

I knew they wouldn't have found anything yet, but I'm still bummed that this case feels like it's at a complete standstill. Unless they can find something, or I can get the facial recognition to work, I'm not sure how to get the answers I need on where Ivy and Valarie went.

"Let me know if you find anything." I plead, "And be careful!"

Kai chuckles, "Always, Lottie-girl. Have fun on your date."

"Yeah, let me know if I need to kick Maverick's ass," Eli adds.

I let them go so they can get ready. Looking at the time, I realize that I need to get ready unless I want to be late.

I shut off the treadmill, grab a towel to wipe my sweat, and head straight for my shower.

The shower takes longer than I intend. I wasn't thinking about having to wash my hair when I took a break from working to work out.

Luckily, I am able to shower myself now, but washing my hair still makes my shoulder sore, probably because it's so long.

By the time I finish the shower and manage to dry and straighten my hair, I only have about ten minutes to eight.

I don't even have time to panic over what I should wear, so I grab the first thing I find. I end up in black skinny jeans, a worn-out band tee that falls off my shoulder, and my typical Vans. I'm sure it's not what Maverick is used to when he goes on a date with a girl, but it's the best I've got.

I finish lacing up my shoes the same second the doorbell rings. I ignore it, figuring someone will get it, but as I'm grabbing my phone and wallet, it rings again and again and again.

Coming downstairs, Cooper and Maverick are nowhere to be found. Swinging the door open reveals Maverick on the front steps, a sunflower in one hand and the other tucked into the pocket of his dark-washed jeans. He wears a blue button-up with the sleeves rolled up to his elbows, showing off the ink on his arms that I want to study more.

His face is pulled into a frown, which is not what I was expecting.

"Do you always open the door without checking first?" He growls. I think that's a new record for me, three seconds in, and he's already annoyed.

I fold my arms across my chest, matching his energy.

"I c-checked."

His eyebrow cocks, "Did you?"

Now that I think about it, I definitely didn't check. It never crossed my mind that I should look before opening the door. But I'll be dammed if I admit that to him.

"Why are you ringing the bell anyway? You *live* here."

"And I told you I'd *pick you up* for our date. I was trying to show you I can be a gentleman."

"Well, that's…sweet." I have to admit. I spent the day thinking this date was more of a joke than anything to him, but already, he's put more effort into it than I expected.

He huffs a laugh, running a hand through his hair and looking back at me.

"I can be sweet when I want to be. Now, do you want your flower or not?" Holding the sunflower out to me, I quickly snatch it from him, making sure he doesn't pull it away.

It's a beautiful sunflower, perfectly bloomed with a neatly trimmed stem. The vibrant yellow is the perfect representation of its name.

"Thanks," I mutter, reluctantly. He got me my favorite flower, and I'm torn, wondering if he chose it himself or if he asked one of his brothers.

He leads me to the car, opening the door and waiting until I'm settled before rounding to his side.

He doesn't say where we're going, and I don't ask; I'm too busy wondering if the radio is turned up enough that he can't hear my heart pounding in my chest the way I can hear it rushing in my ears.

I shouldn't be nervous; this is *Maverick*. He's the only brother that I work with that I'm not in a relationship with, which should make this easy and carefree. So why am I arguing in my head about whether I'm underdressed or not compared to what he showed up in? Does he think that I didn't care enough, and that's why I didn't dress up enough? Or if he's upset about our bickering, and that's why he's so quiet now. Did I ruin this date before it even got a chance to start? Like some sort of twisted self-sabotage.

"I was thinking about a new Korean barbecue place, would you want to try that?" His voice interrupts my inner conflict.

I have no clue what that is. "Sounds good," I say anyway.

Neither of us tries to speak for the rest of the drive, even though it's awkward. I'm grateful because it means I can't say anything stupid or piss him off.

A quiet Charlotte means a happy Maverick.

We arrive at the place, Vagabond. It looks nice from the outside; cool black-and-white modern designs make up the front of the building, and a sleek red sign stands out.

The inside is a large room filled with tables, each housing a small grill in the center. Each table has a fan hood overhead to keep smoke to a minimum, and they're fairly spaced out to feel more private.

The hostess leads us to our table, and I can feel Maverick's hand brushing along the small of my back. It sends a chill up my spine and gives me hope that maybe he's not pissed and I haven't ruined this date before it even began.

We sit on either side of the booth, facing one another. I notice there's only one menu on the table, and it's on his side, so I take a look around, watching different K-Pop music videos play out on any of the many screens placed throughout.

We order drinks, sticking to sodas after last night's fun. Maverick places an order for food, so I'll just have to trust him, since I didn't get to see the menu.

The night's going to be pretty long and awkward if neither of us speaks.

"What made you pick this place?" I ask, startling him as he pulls his focus from one of the many screens around us.

I might be hallucinating, but I think I see a blush spreading across his cheeks.

"Well it had good reviews, people said the food's good." Clearing his throat he adds, "And I knew I could order for you without it seeming barbaric."

That's oddly touching. The fact that he chose this specifically to remove some of my irritational anxiety in a way that doesn't draw attention to it means that he pays attention more than I've realized.

"So, you noticed that I'm a bit incapable of functioning like everyone else?" I feel like making a joke of my quirks will make it easier to address them, but like the other guys, he doesn't go along with my idea of a joke.

"You are capable of doing anything and everything you want to do." He says, quickly adding, "Decision making, however, I will agree, is not your strong suit. I figured this way we wouldn't spend the whole night waiting for you to pick between two dishes when we both know you'd have picked the first of the two choices."

I go to argue, but quickly realize that he's right.

"Am I that predictable?" I ask.

"Yes." He deadpans, "But only with certain things. Other things, like work, for example, your stubbornness replaces your predictability, meaning we never have any clue what you're going to do next. It's amusing and frustrating all in one go."

The waitress comes back, dropping off drinks for us and plates of small appetizers, rice, and raw meat. Leaving without a word, we're left staring at the wide array of food.

Maverick gives a quick description of the complimentary dishes on the table, each one just a small sample of the full dish. Then he shows me what he's chosen: a corn appetizer and fried popcorn chicken. Then for our mains, wine, pork belly, brisket, and some type of chicken.

He urges me to try any of the apps, so I pick a few, taking small bites of the corn and chicken and loving the flavors of each.

He starts grabbing tools from a drawer beside the table, placing pieces of meat on the hot grill between us.

"Oh, and we have to cook our food here, so I thought it'd give me something to do with my hands while we talked, and you wouldn't feel awkward if you were fidgeting with yours." He tells me when he notices me watching him cook.

I stop chewing, mid-bite.

What he said wasn't rude; it was actually very thoughtful. But people usually don't talk so openly about my quirks; it's usually something that's noticed, but swiftly dismissed, or intentionally ignored. My parents always told me that if I gave them attention, then the urge to act them out would only increase, so it was a rule in our house that no one even mentioned them. Even with the other guys, I know they notice, and sometimes they'll even try to intervene, but no one ever mentions a word.

"You just like to lay it all out there, huh?" I force out a laugh, trying to convince myself that his brazen observations of me don't make me want to crawl out of my skin.

He doesn't look up from where he's cooking the food, but he tilts his head.

"In what way?" He asks.

"Just in saying anything about me, or how I act." Pulling on my hands nervously in my lap, I clarify. "No one ever mentions the fact that I twist my fingers, or struggle to pick sometimes, just like Kai and Eli never mentioned anything about me hating crowds and noise after taking me to Myth."

He leaves the meat to cook on the grill, setting down his tools, and he looks everywhere but at me, contemplating.

When his eyes land on mine, I'm instantly rooted in place, unable to move even if I wanted to.

"I just think that ignoring any of it or pretending it's not happening is ignorant. If we don't acknowledge any of it, then how are we supposed to make you more comfortable?"

"But it's n-not any of your jobs to m-make me feel comfortable in n-normal settings," I argue.

"And it's not your job to hide your discomfort to fit in with what everyone else wants to do."

Holy shit.

He reads me like a book; it's unnerving for him to expose me like that, with very little effort on his part. Here I thought that he never gave me a second thought, but in reality, he's been watching me all along. That's the only way he would have observed enough to call me out like this. And he's not even unkind in calling me out, direct, yes, but not rude. He's just very sure of himself, which makes my head spin because I've never felt this seen before.

"I thought you h-hated me." I don't mean to say it, but it's the first thing that comes to mind, and unfortunately, he has me in a spot where my mind is running faster than my mouth, so there's no telling what I'll say.

My eyes widen, and I can feel my face flame, but I manage to keep my eyes on his. He blinks, his eyes dropping back down to the food as he starts flipping pieces, a twitch in his lips.

"No, Charlotte. I never hated you." His eyes fly up to meet mine, "Quite the opposite, actually, which was the problem."

Inside, I'm stumped trying to figure out how Kai and Cooper both were right about him having feelings for me. Outside, I'm holding my breath, waiting for him to explain what he means by that being a problem.

When he doesn't continue, I decide to ask. I've already come this far.

"W-why is that a p-problem?" I have a flash of the conversation that I overheard, and his words that had been a slap in the face that day. "B-because you only s-see me as some k-kid?"

If that's the case, then I don't know what we're doing here. Is this all just some elaborate way of letting me down easy? Would he really go through all of this trouble just to tell me that the thought of being with me is too weird because he only sees me as a kid sister that he has to look out for?

Oh God, what if he decides to tell me that dating his brothers is too complicated and that he's going to have to fire me? Can he even fire me for that? I don't think that's entirely legal, but if he does, then I'm screwed. I'll have no job, and no place to live, and I'd have to go crawling back to my parents. And if I get fired then the case for Ivy and Valarie will go cold because let's face it, none of the guys have the same stubborn drive to sit and stare at a computer for over 60 hours a week to try and piece together the abstract puzzle pieces to lead to one clue that's only one of a million pieces needed to find them. And then I'll not only have let myself down, but also those girls. And I'll have nothing to live for if I lose my guys and all of that.

"Because," He starts, pausing when he can't find the words. "Because I'm your *boss*, I hired you, and you started dating my brothers."

That's not a reason. "And you d-don't want m-me to date your b-brothers?" I ask, confused.

He drops the utensils, shaking his head.

"No, I mean, maybe at first that was the issue. Not because I don't want you to date them, if they make you happy, then that's all that matters." He grows more anxious as he speaks, running his hand through his hair repeatedly.

"If t-that wasn't the p-problem, then w-what was?"

"I'm not sure." He admits softly. "Maybe it was the fact that my brothers were just instantly connected with you, and I was the giant dick that locked you in our office against your will. I thought you were afraid of me, we didn't have the same connection, and when the others talked about dating you, it just felt like they were offering me an in-out of pity."

"And now?" I have to know if he feels differently now, or if he's just jumping into this because he thinks he needs to be around to protect myself and his brothers.

He doesn't answer right away. He takes the time to plate food for both of us, giving me a chance to collect myself so I'm not so much like a live wire ready to burst into flames. But the waiting is also killing me; whatever he says determines how we continue on from here, no pressure or anything.

"Now, I've had a chance to get to know you, on a more personal level, and not just who my brothers describe you as. I've gotten to see your drive and determination at work, and your stubbornness in pretty much every day life. I've seen your true kindness as you've always made an effort to be cordial with me, even when I've been a complete ass to you, and I've gotten to catch glimpses of your attitude that you seem to reserve especially for me."

He pauses, chuckling before his expression sobers into something more serious.

"I've also experienced what it's like to lose you, and while I was able to get to you in time, the sheer panic I felt, not knowing if I'd ever get a chance to see you roll your eyes at me again, or to just man up and stop being afraid of the feelings that I have for you. That was one of the worst experiences of my life, one that I wouldn't wish on my worst enemy. So, I'd be stupid not to own up to the things I said to you in your dorm when you couldn't hear me. I've decided to stop being afraid of things that can make me happy for the simple fact that they can be taken away."

It's like he's reached into my chest and squeezed all the air out of my lungs like two deflating balloons. Once he started, it doesn't seem like he's been able to stop himself, and I'm left drowning in all of the words he's thrown my way. He didn't even throw me a life preserver before chucking me in the deep end, and I have no clue how to respond.

He must take my silence as rejection, quickly picking up his fork to pick at his food.

"If you don't feel that way about me, or if I've done too much to push you away, then I understand." He adds, leaving me to contemplate.

I can't even touch my food, too preoccupied trying to comprehend everything that he just dropped in my lap.

I try to think back to our past interactions, but I have no recollection of him telling me anything that night he came to get me other than to keep my eyes open. Have there really been other signs that I've just missed? He did lock me in the office the first day we met, but that was only because he was looking out for his brothers.

There was the time he kidnapped me from my dorm to take care of me when I was sick, and he also threw away a pan of Mac and cheese because he thought it made me sick. And he's always been very observant, like knowing to take me to the rage room to let off steam, among other times where he's pointed out more than anyone else noticed. I thought he only did that to annoy me, but is it because of his feelings for me?

He said that he's been afraid of things being taken away, which makes sense, knowing how hard his parents' dying took a toll on him. It's obvious that he feels like he has to be the glue that holds everyone together, so I can see him denying himself so his brothers can have what they want.

I just have a tough time fathoming that all four of these men see me as more, and they see past the walls I put up to keep everyone out. But I guess that's one way that Maverick and I are the same: I've never allowed myself to feel for anyone else or let anyone in enough to develop feelings. I know this relationship already is unconventional, and people are going to turn their heads at us like we're crazy, so what's adding one more? I hear what he's saying, and I fully believe every word that he's told me tonight.

I'd be stupid to deny either of us the chance to give this a try because we started off on the wrong foot.

Taking a breath, I steady myself, not wanting to come off as unsure when I tell him, "I w-want to try, i-if you do."

His wide eyes meet mine instantly, shock evident on his face, and now it's his turn to gape like a fish.

"Seriously?"

"Yup," I finally try my food for the first time since he plated it. Flavors explode on my tongue; it's probably the best meat I've ever tried, and I'm not even completely sure what it is.

"So, what do we do from here?" He asked, sounding as confused as I am with the whole situation.

For the first time tonight, I feel pretty content, confused still, but not anxious. Like admitting to the feelings we both have has lifted the dark cloud that follows closely behind me each day, waiting to swoop in and crush me. I have no clue what happens next, but for the first time, I'm okay with the unknown.

Shrugging, I tell him, "Take it day by day. Oh, and we should probably start by telling your brothers that you're all in. I have to make sure they're okay with this."

"This was their idea, so I think they'll be okay with it." He tells me, laughing.

When I can't piece together what he's saying, he lays it out for me.

"Eli and Kai have been trying to get me on board from the beginning. I told them back in the hospital that I wanted in, officially. And the bet was Cooper's idea; he knew you wouldn't back down from a challenge. Trivia night just happened to be a happy coincidence."

Again, I'm left completely dumbfounded at how well they each know me, and touched at how much that shows they care.

Whatever happens with the four of us, I'm ready for it.

18

~ Maverick ~

I don't think I've shared this many emotions since my mother was alive. As much as I miss her, I don't miss this feeling of being completely raw and exposed to anyone else. Regardless, now that the conversation has been had, I'm glad we did it.

Everything is out in the open now, and we can have a fresh start.

I wasn't lying to her; the twins and Coop were fully on board with me telling Charlotte how I feel. Kai had been bugging me about it, making sly comments any chance he got since I admitted it to them in the hospital. And Cooper did playfully suggest baiting her into a date with me. I just happened to luck out that he decided to go out and get drunk at trivia night, because it presented the perfect opportunity that led us here.

We kept the rest of dinner pretty light, small talk, and only surface-level topics.

She seems completely relaxed as we eat, other than a couple of sideways looks at some of the food I urge her to try.

I'm glad that I chose this place. I had a feeling that the overall atmosphere would put her at ease, and I was right. Eliminating the choices for her and making it a less formal dining experience really did help her relax and not overthink everything so much.

She was very unique, and finding ways to make everyday situations less stressful for her was an accomplishment I'm going to aim to achieve much more of.

Our only other misstep through the whole meal comes when she offers to pay for half. She tried to ignore my death stare until it was too uncomfortable for even the waiter to stand, finally caving and agreeing to put her stupid card away.

The night started out so tense, but it's much more laid back now, and I'm not ready for it to end.

Leaving the restaurant, I check that she's okay with going somewhere else. When she agrees, I head straight for my favorite spot.

Traffic isn't too bad for a Saturday night, and we have a pretty calm drive back across town towards Riverside.

I'm mesmerized watching her face light up as she takes in the skyline, lit against the evening sky. The bright blue lights from the Acosta and Main Street bridges reflect off the water, creating a stunning landscape.

There are a lot of hidden gems in Jax that many people don't know about. The riverwalk is a good one, the Friendship Fountain, and a variety of public parks to enjoy the river. Under the Dames Point bridge, though, there's a secluded park that has the most gorgeous views of the river, and you can look down the river to see all of downtown lit up against the night sky. On really nice days, you can catch the manatees as they swim by as well, but it may be too cold to find any just yet.

I had overheard Kai talking about how much she enjoyed the river walk with him, and I know she's gone for runs along the water many days at work when she needed a break. So hopefully, this was a good choice for our first date. I didn't want to take her anywhere else that was going to be overcrowded and rowdy; I'd rather have a chance to hear some of the thoughts that go through her head.

Parking the car, I help her out, keeping her hand in mine as we make the short walk into the park. There are small light posts just off the water, lighting up the path past the playground and the El Faro memorial. We keep walking until we reach the small pier built to take us out over the water, adjacent to the bridge.

The pier has no lights, giving us the perfect opportunity to see the stars in the night sky and the headlights passing overhead.

This park has only been around for a couple of years, and it's not as popular as others because it's so far north in the city, away from most of the day-to-day businesses.

"How'd you find this place?" Her small voice breaks up the silence between us.

"I used to try to take Zeus to a new park every weekend, just to burn off some of his energy. He didn't like this one much, but it stuck with me."

"It's so quiet, I like it." She watches the bridge, staring at the cars passing by without a care in the world.

The way the moon reflects off her face, upturned towards the sky, makes her look like she just stepped out of her own romcom movies. Straight off the screen and by my side.

"Kai said you like the riverwalk," I comment, "Do you like that specifically or nature in general?"

She chews her lip, her head tilts to the side, causing her hair to slip off her shoulder, showing me the skin that's been painfully on display all night.

"I like being outdoors, within reason." She hesitates, laughing to herself. "I don't like hiking, or anything outdoors that I might encounter creepy crawlers or snakes…but the riverwalk, and this? This is nice."

That makes a lot of sense for her, loves the beauty of nature, but only when there's no hidden threats to worry about.

"We'll have to come back during the day sometime, then you can see all the manatees swim by, and if you're lucky, you might even spot a dolphin too. As long as that's not too scary for you?" I can't help but pick on her;

it's just so much fun to see the irritation take over her usually soft features.

In a very surprising act, she spins, placing both hands on my chest and shoving me towards the water. I don't move more than an inch from her force, but the attempt is so adorable. Like a cute baby raccoon fighting over the last handful of food.

Swooping down, I wrap my arms around both of her legs, lifting her up and setting her on the railing. I make sure to push her to the edge so she feels off balance.

Immediately, her legs wrap around my waist, and her hands fist my shirt, holding on for dear life.

"That wasn't very nice," I tell her, watching her adjust her hands to keep a hold of me.

"S-s-sorry."Her eyes are wide with fear, and I relish the feeling that she has to rely on me to keep her from crashing into the river. Not that I would ever let her fall, but I don't need to tell her that right now.

Dragging it out, I pretend to think about it.

"I don't know, I don't think sorry is going to cut it."

"What do you want?" She's quick to make an offer, knowing how this game goes.

"Hmm," Tapping my chin, I think. Her legs shift around my waist, making me feel off balance with the strength she uses to pull me towards her.

I lean forward, and she pulls at my neck to keep herself up until we're chest to chest.

"How about a kiss?" We're close enough that I can feel her breath brushing against my lips, but I still want her to choose to give it to me.

Her eyes linger on my lips, snapping back to mine like she can't fight the pull. A quiet breath passes before her tongue glides over her lip, slow, deliberate – tempting.

Without warning, she pushes forward, sealing her lips with mine.

It's like nothing I've ever experienced before. Her lips on mine are like a gentle, soft wave reaching the shore. They build up only to softly crash, leaving a warm feeling in my chest. Kissing her feels whole, like the last piece I was missing has finally found its way home.

I'm kicking myself for denying wanting her for as long as I have, if this is what I've been missing out on.

Her hips start to rock, instantly bringing my cock to life. Reluctantly, I pull back from the kiss, not wanting to take this any further tonight, especially not on the damn pier.

She's flushed and breathless, not as concerned with falling in the water now, but still clinging to me. Her lips are swollen, and the blacks of her eyes are dilated to the point I can hardly see the hazel color anymore.

I can't help but steal one more quick kiss before untangling myself from her, setting her gently back on the dock.

She follows back to the car, seemingly in a daze.

We ride back to the house with the windows down and the radio turned up. She keeps her hand out the window, surfing the wind while she hums along to any of the songs she knows on my playlist, which I begrudgingly added some Taylor Swift songs to just for her. I won't ever admit it, but some of them aren't that bad.

When we pull up to the house, Cooper meets us at the front door.

"Aww, you two are holding hands! I take it the date went well?" Without waiting for a response, he slaps me on the shoulder. "Way to pull your head out of your ass, finally."

He tosses an arm over her shoulder, dragging her towards the living room.

"To celebrate, I picked a rom-com for us and have ice cream ready to go in the freezer."

She turns on her heel, slipping from under his arm to rush back over to me.

Pushing up on her tiptoes, she presses a kiss to my cheek.

"I had a r-really fun t-time. Thank you."

"You're welcome, go enjoy your ice cream." With a final squeeze, I send her back over to Cooper, waiting in the doorway. The two of them launch themselves onto the couch, dragging blankets over them and getting situated for their movie.

I head upstairs, ready to wash off the day and take care of the blue balls that I've been sporting since the pier.

Even still, I can't wipe the smile off my face, knowing that I finally got my girl.

19

~ Charlotte ~

I love work.

I know that's not something people normally say, but in my case, I love my job. I get to do something I love all day, without even having finished college.

I guess that's a perk of dating your bosses.

But today, rather than getting lost in a sea of codes and cold trails to finding Ivy and Valarie, I'm selfishly thinking about my date with Maverick. I'm still shocked by how well it went, and despite him trying to throw me in the river, we still managed to have our first kiss.

He was like a completely different person on our date, finally having dropped his asshole façade to talk about his feelings. I'm sure it was painful for him, but I'm glad that he pulled it off. One of us had to…and better him than me.

Kai and Eli were on their way home, and I was hoping they had found something, anything, to help with the case, because my motivation was slowly dying out the more days I spent looking at a screen with no answers.

Speak of the devils, my office door flies open, slamming into the wall, and Kai comes barreling through.

"Lottie-girl!" He spins my chair around to face him, laying a kiss on me before pushing my chair to spin again while he drops into one of the chairs. "I missed you so much."

Eli follows him into the room at a much more reasonable pace while I work on getting my chair to stop spinning and back into its original spot.

He, too, comes over to place a kiss on my forehead, thankfully not touching my chair. "How was your weekend?" He asks, taking the seat next to Kai.

"It was good, I had a fun time Saturday night, and yesterday we just stayed in."

"Sure, rub it in that while we were stuck in Georgia, you were going out on dates and living your best life." Kai sulks, "No offense, babe, but I *hate* Georgia."

I wave him off, not caring whether he loves or hates it. I don't live there anymore, and I haven't considered it my home for years now.

"Did you find anything?" I ask hopefully.

"Possibly," Eli hedges. Pulling out his phone, he shows me a picture. The quality is pretty low, and the photo is dark, but I've been staring at grainy security footage for weeks now, so I instantly recognize the face in the phone.

"That's the guy." I look between the two of them, and back down to the picture, making sure I'm seeing what I think I am.

The very man I've been trying to ID for weeks from security footage is in the picture on Eli's phone, meaning that he was there.

"It is indeed," Kai agrees, clicking his tongue before delivering the punchline of this fucked up joke. "Good news is that he does still work there, bad news is that no one would give us any information on him, and when he caught wind of us asking and hanging around, he fled."

"Not even a name?" I ask dejectedly, already knowing his answer before he says anything.

"Only a first name, Beck." He says, shaking his head.

"We couldn't really figure out what his official position in the bar is." Eli adds, "It was strange, he was kind of just there, not really working any one position."

"So you think he might be the manager?" I guess.

"I think it's worth a shot to look into. It's about all we have to go off of right now."

I let my head drop back, landing on the back of my chair, the mental exhaustion weighing heavily on me just thinking about the next rabbit hole I'm about to dive into.

"Thank you both for going."

"Anything for you, Lottie-girl," Kai winks. "Though I'd say that you owe us another date." His eyebrows bounce up and down, Eli shaking his head next to him.

"I think that can be arranged, but not today." With that, they clear out of my office, making excuses about their own work or needing to go home to sleep and shower. Really, I think they know that I'm about to dive into my computer, unable to emerge for hours, until I either find something or can't take it anymore.

Once they leave, I settle in, getting comfortable for the long afternoon ahead while I try to find everything I can about anyone who owns or runs the Tilted Kilt in any way.

Getting information on the employees registered as working there isn't hard, but digging into ownership and management is more challenging because businesses are bought and sold all the time without proper documentation of the parties involved. People also get promoted or inherit things, which also isn't as easy to find.

I use the same method I used when I hacked into their security system to see the footage, but this time I try to look at the live feeds to see if I can at least find this Beck anywhere. Of course, being the middle of the day, it looks like they only have a skeleton crew on hand.

Flipping through the cameras, I realize two things: I don't have the ability to move any of them to change the view, and I'm stuck with wherever the cameras are already pointed. And there are no cameras in any of the offices laid out in the back of the bar, not that I figured I'd be that lucky. Anything I find has to be visible in the bar's main areas.

It's not ideal, but at least I have something to look into instead of following the same cold trails.

I leave the feeds up and set it to record, so anything I'm not watching live I can play back later. I pull up a new tab, trying to find any records I can on the bar's history. I'm able to see a plethora of things, from liquor orders, license history, earnings documents, and police reports filed at that address.

The police reports from when both Ivy and Valarie went missing are in there, each with minimal details and quickly closed without further investigation. It seems the police weren't interested in the abduction spot for their reports.

And this is why they're no longer working this case.

I know I'm not an expert, but I think the spot where two people went missing should be looked into a bit further, not just by showing up and asking if they were there.

I spend a few hours running every name I can find in the notes for the bar through LexNex – a police system used for identification purposes, it at least lets me see a driver's license photo, so I can try to match Beck to one of them. If that's even his real name, the gut feeling I have is that it's not. But once I get through this list, I can start checking each person's personal history to try to dig up any connections they have to our mystery man.

The sun is setting, shining through the curtains into my office, and by the time I sit back to take a break and stretch. The list has given me nothing so far, just a bunch of old men who, from what I can tell, just like to invest money in small businesses.

My back cracks like popcorn when I stretch, and I slowly sink into my chair, savoring the loose feeling that follows.

It's quickly washed away when I see something move out of the corner of my eye.

"Fuck!" I jump so high that I slip out of the chair, slipping to the floor. I try to control my breathing, shooting daggers at Cooper, who is doing his best to control his laughter, watching me from the edge of his seat in front of my desk.

"I would apologize, but I've been here for about an hour now." He holds his hands up in a 'what can I do way', "You were locked in, didn't pay me any attention."

"Well, the heart palpitations certainly caught my attention." Dropping back onto the floor, I close my eyes and relish the feeling of just existing. I'm too tired to pull myself back up.

I feel his presence looming over me, cracking an eye open, I see his amused grin staring back at me.

"Are you ready to call it a night so I can drive you home?"

"Not even close," I groan. "But we might as well go before your brothers come barreling through the door."

Grabbing my hand, he helps ease me up from the floor. "That's probably a good call. Kai has been blowing up our group chat, threatening to come pick you up if I can't get you out of here soon."

"Hm, I would have guessed Maverick." I shrug, packing my bag.

"Normally I'd agree, but he's been in such a good mood since your *date* the other night that he hasn't quite shifted back into his overbearing self."

"It was a lot of fun." Leaving the office, it's much darker than I thought; it seems that I really lost track of time. I'm surprised Kai didn't come back for me.

When we get home, the house is lit up. I can see Maverick in the kitchen through the front windows, cooking dinner. I can also see feet over the back of the couch. I think it's safe to assume that'd be Kai.

It's still surreal to think that I get to live here with four amazing men who have done nothing but prove how much they care about me. I've felt more welcome in this house than I ever did in my home growing up.

Fresh aromas of pasta and bread fill the house, making my mouth water as we step through the door. Getting lost in my computer meant skipping meals, and my stomach is reminding me that all I've had today is a couple of energy drinks and air.

The table is set, pasta, sauce, fresh-baked bread, and grated cheese fill the space. Maverick's just finished pouring water into the waiting glasses when he notices our arrival.

"You're just in time," He tells us, yelling over his shoulder for Kai and Eli, "Food's ready!"

Cooper takes my bag off my shoulder for me, and Maverick ushers me to my seat, pulling my chair out while I sit.

Zeus comes running from the back door, where Eli is stepping inside. Sprinting to my side, he sits his head in my lap, his tail swishing from side to side, looking for pets.

Maverick takes the seat to my right, per usual, and tries to call Zeus off to his bed, receiving an adorable pout in return. Ultimately, he stays with his head on my leg, keeping me warm and waiting for scraps while I eat.

Kai hops over the couch, stealing the seat to my left, leaving Cooper and Eli to the other side. He takes a look at the table, eyes widening, but just as quickly, his face crumbles into a mask of confusion.

"Why is the sauce on the side?" He asks, looking to Maverick.

Eli pauses with his fork halfway to his mouth, a full plate already in front of him being devoured. "Who cares? Just eat it."

"But he always makes it in one pot, it's how mom did it."

Maverick's fork drops to the table. "I made it this way so Charlotte can choose how much sauce she'd like. Now, can you just eat your food, please?

Warmth blooms in my chest, remembering his words at dinner the other night, and actually loving that he's making it a point for my quirks to be heard and not weird.

Dinner is delicious, and I'm able to make a plate with mostly buttered noodles, with just a spoonful of sauce on the side, mostly to dip the bread in. Maverick apparently has a hobby of baking sourdough, and today's recipe is a pesto mozzarella bread that makes me want to die; it's so good.

Every day, I learn new things about each of them that make my heart beat just a little faster in my chest. It feels like I'll never know everything there is to know about each of them, but at least that means I shouldn't ever get bored.

Cooper and I washed up the dishes once everyone's finished, having been the last two home, it felt right to offer.

I'm met with unhappy grunts and complaints when I decline after-dinner movies and ice cream, and I need to head upstairs to check in on the cameras I pulled from the bar. As it gets later, my chances of catching a glimpse of Beck rise.

There's a tick in Maverick's jaw, and I brace myself for him to make a fuss about me working after hours. To my surprise, he lets me go without a fight, urging Kai and Eli to do the same.

When I pull up the footage from the bar, it's noticeably more crowded now than it was when I pulled it up hours ago. It would be hard to spot the one person I'm looking for with the wide view of the bar, but I keep it up on my spare monitor while I open up the LexNex software again, ready to jump back in where I left off.

What feels like hours later, I finally get one tiny grain of hope in the form of a personal history cross-match.

Digging through all of the legal paperwork that I could gather on the bar, I found a signature of Gregory Fisher. Working down my list, I searched for his name, found his personal documentation, and saw that he was one of two owners of the Tilted Kilt as of 2012. None of the paperwork indicates that there have been any new owners or changes in power since then.

Pulling the identification for Gregory in LexNex, I'm able to pull his photo ID. He's not very impressionable, an older white man, with salt-and-pepper hair that's on the far side of gray than black at this point. If I passed him on the street, I wouldn't remember his face.

In his information, however, I can see a list of immediate family members, especially if they live in the same residence or are on the same phone plan, or anything like that.

Within his immediate family, there are only three members: KellyAnn, who I'm assuming is his wife, based on the age; Sierra, who would be a daughter; and one Beckett Fisher.

I don't want to get my hopes up, but it's hard not to when I've been looking for a Beck tied to the bar, and now I'm presented with a Beckett. The odds are too good not to be true.

Immediately, I plug his name and age into the system to run another check, holding my breath as it spools and searches.

And just like magic, my luck holds. Popping up on the screen, the results appear. Beckett Fisher, 32 years old, acting manager of The Tilted Kilt, is listed as the sole inheritor of the bar, to be agreed upon, or, if need be, due to the untimely deaths of either owner.

Eagerly clicking on the photo ID, I nearly jump out of my seat when his face fills the screen. A perfect match to the photo on Eli's phone, and to the grainy screenshot I stole off their saved footage ages ago.

Finally, I've been digging and digging, and now I at least have one small victory to show for it, to give some indication that there is more to be figured out here, and I'm on the right track. This is what I needed to reignite my determination.

Now that I have him identified, I make sure to pull up both feeds where he could be seen with Ivy and Valarie, take screenshots of each, and send them to my printer along with his ID and background.

The screenshots have timestamps, indicating they were taken the night each of the girls went missing. And his ID verifies that the person in the photos is indeed him, giving something concrete to question.

Along with seeing if I could find any way to link him to the posting I'd found about Ivy, and searching to make sure there were no posts about Valerie, we would need to question him. We needed to see if we could catch him in a lie or just get some understanding of why he was the last person seen with either girl before they went missing.

It was nothing more than a suspicion at this point, but it was all I got.

A knock at the door makes me jump, spinning to check the door. When I do, I notice the room is full of light… sunlight. That would mean that I got so caught up that I forgot to sleep last night.

Maverick's head pokes around the door, noticing my perfectly made bed before finding me at my desk.

"I was about to head over to the office and wanted to see if you needed a ride," He trails off, giving me a once-over. "But I take it you're not going today?"

Right, the office. I should go; the drive there would give me a mental break, and the change of scenery would help keep/ my mind focused on work.

"I'm going, I just need to change." I try to step around him, heading for my closet to grab a fresh set of clothes, but he stops me with a hand on my bicep.

I stare at his hand before looking up to meet his eyes, raising a brow in question.

"Did you sleep at all last night?" He asks, studying my face.

"Maybe?" Shrugging, I try to step away, avoiding eye contact so he doesn't know I'm full of shit. Though he probably already does.

"Charlotte," He sighs, sounding like a disappointed parent.

I don't let him finish that thought, finally trying out standing up for myself with the small sliver of comfort that he might be too proud of me to be upset.

"Maverick, I've told you before that I'm an a-adult. If I need to sleep, I will, but right now I need to get to the office to go over what I found with all of you so we can figure out what to do next."

His face turns sour, the vein in his forehead starting to pulse a little bit, something I haven't seen in a while with his newfound nice side. He studies my face, and I force myself to meet his eyes while he does, not willing to let him act like I'm a child needing to adhere to a schedule.

"So, you found something?" He finally relents, releasing my arm and crossing his.

Nodding, I don't offer up anything more, darting into the closet to change.

"I'm leaving in five minutes, be ready or I'm dragging you out of the house in whatever you've got on." He threatens, closing the door behind him.

That's the Maverick I'm used to; it's good to see that he hasn't totally lost his attitude.

He gave me five minutes, but I'm ready in three. Throwing on leggings and a hoodie, hair tossed into a messy bun, and teeth brushed, I'm downstairs waiting by the door while he grabs the keys to lock up.

Nervous energy buzzes through my veins, but it's not my usual anxiety. I'm eager to share what I've found and make a plan to hopefully get us one step closer to finding the girls.

I just hope this doesn't end up in another disappointing dead end, because I'm running out of options to look into, and I'm not sure where else I could go from here.

20

~ Charlotte ~

Once we get to GLS, I'm out of the car as soon as it's in park, hearing Maverick mutter curses behind me as he follows just a step behind.

Sascha isn't in her usual spot behind the front desk, and I'm too thankful not to have to see her to question why she isn't here. I beeline straight to my office, tossing my bag onto my chair and plugging my laptop into my monitors, pulling out the papers I printed at home.

Maverick leans against the wall just inside the door, pocketing his phone moments before the other three join us, varying looks of confusion and interest on their faces.

Cooper leans against the windowsill while Kai and Eli take both of the chairs. None of them speaks, watching me lay out all of my things, they wait.

"So, I was working on running through the list I had from names tied to the bar last night," I summarize while pulling all the programs up on my computer, splitting them between monitors so everything is visible at once.

"While I was doing that, I came across one of the owners of the bar, Gregory Fisher." I pull his photo to the forefront of my screen, turning it so they all can see. "While I was checking his information, I came up with three family members: his wife, daughter, and son – Beckett Fisher."

"Beck?" Eli asks, sitting up in his seat, recognizing the name.

Without a word, I push the printed papers to the edge of the desk, showing them the ID and the screenshots.

They all lean in, taking a closer look.

"Well, shit." Kai breathes, studying the photos.

"Yeah," I agree. "So now we have a name to match the face last seen with both of the girls on the nights they vanished. I even pulled the timestamps, which match the date and time listed in both police reports. But neither report says anything about him being questioned at the time of the reports, even though he's listed as the acting manager and he was clocked in to work both nights."

"The cops didn't question him at all?" Maverick asks.

Shaking his head, Eli answers for me. "No, when you sent us on that first assignment, we read over the reports. They were bare boned at best. The only people they talked to were the friends, and even that was laughable, how little was asked."

"They didn't talk to anyone who worked there to see if they saw anything?" Cooper asks.

"Not according to the reports."

I flip through the saved videos I pulled from the feeds, finding one from the night Valerie went missing.

"I don't have a lot of visibility of the bar from their cameras, but I did find one clip where the cops can be seen." Pointing at the screen, I show them in the far corner, where an officer can be seen approaching the bartender, who is washing glasses. "It looks like he was asking questions, or trying to, but look here, his partner comes over, and within seconds they're leaving the bar."

"Did you try to ID that officer?" Maverick interjects.

"No, I haven't gotten that far; it took me longer than I expected to find out who owns the place and who's in charge on a day-to-day basis."

"You think that whoever is behind this has inside help?" Cooper guesses, "Someone to cover their tracks and make sure the reports are closed without ever really being looked into?"

Maverick nods, not looking away from the screen.

"It makes sense," Kai agrees, "All the cases are bound to go cold if there's no suspects to look into, and no indication of foul play."

"What do you want to do from here?" Maverick directs the question to me, looking tense. He finally tears his eyes away from the screen.

The nerves slam into me like a brick wall. Suddenly, I'm at a pivotal point of having to make a choice. Do we focus on looking into the cop from the feeds? Or do we set our sights on Beck? Neither one will give us the full picture, but splitting our time between the two could take longer in the grand scheme of things. I don't want to make the wrong call and cost us more time, still not knowing where the girls are.

My legs start to shake, bouncing off the floor under my chair. I knead my hands together, needing the comforting feeling of fidgeting to ground me.

"Is there any way that we can get Beck in for questioning? If anything, just to ask him about his interaction with the girls?"

Maverick contemplates, running his hand over his jaw.

"I can talk to the Sheriff, see if he can help us get some type of warrant to bring him in. But we'd have to set it up with the police department up in Georgia; there's no way that JSO will have jurisdiction, even with the girls being from here, they were taken up there, and that's where the cases were initially opened."

Processing that, I try to think of other angles that need to be covered. We have to work blind, hoping that we can get what we need to get Beck alone.

"I think t-that Eli and Kai need to go back t-to the b-bar." I take a breath, trying to steady myself and control the stutter. "I think we need to keep a close eye on Beck while we try to see if I can link him to the listing that I found, which will give us more leverage, combined with the screenshots. And we need to make sure he doesn't s-slip away with anyone else."

Kai's head drops back in the chair, and a groan tears from his chest.

"I really hate Georgia."

"Oh, suck it up." Cooper reaches over to slap the back of his head.

"If I can prove that he had anything to do with Ivy ending up on the dark web, then that would mean grounds to search his computer, right?" I ask Maverick, my mind racing with every possible option.

"It'd be pretty hard to argue, and almost impossible to deny if you can find that," Cooper confirms.

I can see Maverick's jaw grinding. I know he hates the idea of me dealing with anything on the dark web; it's the whole reason he shut this down in the first place. But at this point, he has to see that it's inevitable if we want to get any answers.

"Then I think that I should go with you two up to Georgia." I tell Kai and Eli, "The closer we are to keeping watch while I try to work this out, the better. And if we can get the warrant, then you two can come up and meet us there, we can question Beck and see where that leads us." I look between Cooper and Maverick, hoping like hell neither of them has any objections.

Maverick, of course, looks like he has plenty. I guess being difficult is his forte.

"I think we all should stay far away from that place until we know if we have any solid ground to stand on. Why are we going to put ourselves close to something shady on a hope and a prayer that we can get in to get information?"

"Ivy went missing two months ago, Valerie one month ago." I list off, "If this is some kind of pattern that he's working, then that would only mean he's going to find someone else to take, and probably soon. It's better we be there for it to have solid evidence rather than add another file to our pile of missing persons." I try my best to keep my frustration locked away, but the sheer thought of it is driving my panic higher and higher. I need to control my emotions and not give him any indication that this is a bad idea. I know it's a solid train of thought, and while it might scare him, we can't do everything we need to from behind a screen.

"That's all the more reason for *you* to be nowhere near him!"

"I'll be with Kai and Eli the whole time. I'll be working my end of things from my computer, and I won't be in any danger of getting grabbed, if that's what you're worried about." I stand my ground. I won't have this case taken away from me again. He can either get on board and offer the help I need, or I'll do it myself. Only one of those outcomes puts me at a significantly higher risk.

The others watch us, the tension building like a tea kettle on the stove, ready to burst at any moment.

"You're so fucking *stubborn*." He growls, but I can see his defenses dropping down, giving me that glimmer of hope.

"If I recall, y-you said t-that you like my s-stubbornness." And there's that sass that he says I save especially for him. He's not wrong, but he just has a way of dragging it out of me. Before I met him, I never knew it was there. I was afraid of my own shadow, and I would have never dared to poke at anyone the way I do him.

"*Fine*." He caves, "But the three of you are there to work on finding what you can and *observing*. Do not approach him, even if you see something; just get the evidence that you can and wait for us. I want updates on anything you find. If you find that he's looking at furry porn in his free time, then I want to know, but you do *nothing*. Are we clear?"

I'm sure my face reflects my disgust. Kai and Eli fall into fits of laughter, but Maverick's gaze never strays from mine, waiting for an answer.

"Okay." If it means him dropping the fight of letting us go, then I'll agree to it. But if it comes down to it, I won't let another girl disappear.

"Alright, then I'll get started reaching out to the sheriff." Without another word, he leaves the room, allowing me to sink into my seat, feeling the weight of the morning land heavily on my shoulders.

"Way to go, Lottie." Kai praises me. "I never thought I'd see you stand up to Mav, but you did it."

"It helps that he's already whipped, not even a week into admitting his shit," Eli adds, both of them snickering like children.

"All right, you two go get whatever you need sorted out so you can head out." Cooper insists, shooing them both out of the room.

Shutting the door behind them, he turns to face me. Stepping around the desk, he pulls me up into his chest, crushing me in his arms.

"Are you sure you want to do this?" He asks, pulling away to see my face.

With him, I don't feel immediately defensive. He isn't asking to try and talk me out of anything; he genuinely wants to check in, always sensing when my anxiety is ramping up. And going head-to-head with Maverick is a sure-fire way to send my nerves over the edge.

"I need to do this," I tell him, and I mean it. I've already invested so much in this, and I won't throw it all away now just because it's starting to feel real, that we could actually be getting somewhere.

"I know, I just want to understand why." I don't understand what he's asking. This is the job that we all signed up for. Why else would I want to figure this out?

"Why do you feel so strongly about this case in particular?" He continues when I don't respond. "We deal with a lot of missing persons cases, and it's always sad when we don't get the answers we want, or any answers at all. But since you started on this, you've had such a hungry desire to figure it all out; hell, you've lost so much sleep over this case. I just want to know, why this one?"

Dropping my head to his chest, I think it over. I can admit that he might be right. I have hyper-focused on this since Eli reached out to me for help. But it made me feel needed, and this case has given me an opportunity to apply the skills I've spent years learning to something more meaningful than some shabby side gigs, like programming software for faceless companies. This has meaning; it's someone's life.

"I've always been good at what I've taught myself. Computers have always made sense to me, and I've always gotten a rush using them to piece together information that normally wouldn't make sense. And for as long as I can remember, I've been told that my skills are nothing but a waste." Flashes of my parents' insults run through my mind, but I shake them away, forcing them down into that locked box inside my mind. "I know how it feels to be invisible, like I could disappear tomorrow and the world would keep turning without pause. Wondering if anyone would bat an eye if they never saw me again. That's a lonely feeling; one I wouldn't wish on anyone. When I think of those girls, that's the one thing that comes to mind: they're probably terrified going through whatever they're going through. To think that they might feel like they've been forgotten, that they're invisible now, even to the people they love, that makes me sick to my stomach to even consider. I've lived it, without ever having been taken. And I know that if I were to disappear, I would hope that someone was fighting like hell to get me back. That's why I can't give it up. If I don't keep pushing, then who will?"

I can feel his heart pounding in his chest, speeding up with every word.

He pulls me closer, crushing me again until it's hard to breathe.

"You're not invisible, Charlotte. We would go to the ends of the Earth to find you if you ever disappeared on us. You know that, right?"

My lips curve into a smile because I know he's right. I might have been alone for a long time, but I'm far from it now.

"I know, and I love that you would."

He brings his lips to mine, forcing every bit of love and passion into the kiss, and he tells me again, without words this time, how strongly he feels.

All too soon, he pulls away, leaving me lightheaded and breathless.

"Remember what Maverick said, just don't put yourself at risk and keep us in the loop." He steals another kiss, finally retreating towards the door. My body racked with shivers at the loss of his warmth.

He doesn't wait for a response, leaving me alone in my office to calm my racing heart.

While I'll do everything in my power to find the girls, I'll also do what I need to make it back home to my guys.

I've just gotten them, and I refuse to lose them.

21

~ Kai ~

Have I mentioned how much I hate Georgia?

Their football team, their interstates, their drivers; all of it. I'm not a fan. Of course, that's where we're needed to figure out this fucked up case.

My only saving grace was that it took us three days to get up here. Charlotte is already enrolled in online courses, so she was ready to go right away, but Eli and I had to get special permission to complete our coursework virtually for the time being. It was our last semester, and as much as we wanted to get to the bottom of the missing girls, we wanted to make it to graduation just as much.

Another perk is that Lottie's here with us this time, so it won't feel as torturous missing her, and we upgraded from our usual motel to a comfortable hotel suite. We needed plenty of room for Eli and Lottie's equipment, and space for Coop and Mav if and when they needed to come up.

I do feel more worthless, being cooped up in the room while they both type away, using their tech skills to dig up anything they can find. I obviously know how to use a computer, but my skills are more geared towards online gaming than towards hacking and programming.

They both tell me that being here for support is all they need, but until we can get out and actually start looking for something, I'm just a sitting duck. The only helpful thing I've been assigned to do is watch the bar's security feeds each night, hoping to catch a glimpse of Beck.

I pull the container of noodles from the microwave, just about the only thing we can make in here besides cereal, carrying it over to where Lottie's set up at the second desk they dragged into the living room.

She's hunched over, staring intently at the screen, and I take a moment to just appreciate her beauty. Even in worn-out sweats, and her hair falling out of the bun it's been in for days, and her glasses perched on the end of her nose, she takes my breath away. I love the way the light from the screen highlights the freckles that dust her cheeks. I can only ever catch them when I'm up close, but I've probably counted them a thousand times, committing each one to memory.

"Here," I make my presence known, not wanting to scare her. Sitting the bowl down next to her keyboard, her face lights up at the sight of it.

"Thanks." She smiles warmly up at me, using the interruption to pull off her glasses, rubbing at her eyes and blinking as she takes in the room, as if seeing it for the first time.

She lunges for the fork, shoveling a pile of steaming noodles into her mouth.

"What time is it?" Her words are muffled by the food so much that I barely understand her.

Laughing, I reach out to catch the broth sliding down the side of her chin, earning another smile in return.

"It's just after seven," I tell her.

Her eyes widen, pausing mid-chew.

"PM?"

"Yeah, you two have been at it for a while. Though Eli tapped out about an hour ago." Nodding my head, I indicate my brother, currently passed out with his face on his keyboard, glasses askew, and burger wrappers surrounding his workstation.

"Sorry?" She looks sheepishly at me, quickly diving back into her food.

"No worries, I knew that you two were going to be busy. And I've managed to keep myself entertained for the most part. Anything new on your end?" I ask.

"Nothing yet, I'm still trying to locate and trace the origins of the posting, but it's like trying to find a needle in a haystack, and the haystack is also full of other decoy needles, and I'm just getting poked and stabbed repeatedly."

"Sounds painful," I cringe at the analogy. I don't envy either of their jobs, having to make something out of nothing. I'm much happier being the one to just swoop in for the hands-on activities.

She nods, finishing her noodles and leaning back in the chair. Stretching out, her t-shirt rides up, flashing me a sliver of her stomach in the process.

"What if we take a break?" I can already see her arguments building, excuses of needing to keep working and not being able to stop until she finds what she needs. "You're going to get burnt out if you keep staring at that screen, as something new will magically appear. Just one night," I offer. "We can even go to the bar and check it out, call it recon, just live and in person instead of watching the feeds."

I'm hoping that if I make it sound like work, then I can convince her to step away.

I can see how much she needs a break, and I'd be lying if I said I didn't have Maverick blowing up my phone, checking in on her every chance he gets.

He might have been able to hide his overbearing tendencies so she doesn't notice them as much, but he's still the same old Maverick, trying to control everything, even from home. If I didn't know him any better, I'd be insulted by the way he keeps sending me reminders to make sure she's eating and sleeping, but I know it's just because he cares.

"I guess… " She heaves a breath, quickly adding, "As long as we're there to work, and keep an eye out."

"Yes!" Jumping up, I bounce around, eager for the chance to get out of here, waking Eli in the process.

He sits up, looking around, confused, squinting at us until he finds his glasses and pushes them back into place.

"What's happening?" His voice is still heavy with sleep, but he's more alert, standing up to stretch.

I grab Lottie by the shoulders, dragging her from her chair and pushing her towards her room to get dressed.

"We're getting out, going to the bar for recon." Heading into my own room, I yell over my shoulder. "Get dressed! We're leaving in twenty!" Slamming the door, I don't give him a chance to argue, digging through my suitcase, I find jeans and a button-up, perfect casual attire for the night.

I'm ready to go in record time, waiting in the living room for the other two.

Eli is just behind me, stepping out in his signature ripped jeans and a matching black tee. His hair is still wet, indicating that he finally did take a shower.

Luckily, he doesn't bring up any arguments about getting out for the night. By the look on his face, I'd say he's relieved to get to step away from the computer for a while.

Lottie steps out of her room, wearing the same little black dress and Vans from the night we all went to Myth, instantly taking me back. It seems like forever ago; all of us have changed so much in such a short amount of time.

It's the same dress, but she looks much different in it this time. Not as skittish and shy, she wears her newfound confidence like a supermodel, looking so sexy, it hurts.

Even with the new confidence around us, her hands still fist in front of her, unable to stand still while our eyes rake over her.

Eli steps up to her, prying her hands apart to take one in his, spinning her around to get a full view of the dress.

He leans in, brushing his lips against hers.

"Stunning," He whispers, and we both watch her cheeks blush red.

I know other people would look at our situation and wonder how I could stand here and watch my brother being affectionate with my girl, and I get it, it's not for everyone. But when I look at them, all I see is the love they share for one another, and the affection and admiration in his eyes when he's close to her.

Knowing Lottie as long as I have, I know that her heart is bigger than anyone else I've ever met. There's plenty of room for myself and my brothers, and we all return the same love for her. So, I'm not jealous; I'm thankful that she has all of us to lean on when she needs to, and we're all here by her side to help and protect her.

He steps back, giving me room to step into her, stealing my own kiss.

"What he said." Winking, I run a finger over her cheek, feeling the heat from the blush as I do.

"T-thanks." She tucks a strand of hair behind her ear, looking both of us over. "Y-you two both look really n-nice."

"Well, we have to clean up if we're going to be next to you all night." I link an arm with her, pulling her from the room before she can change her mind.

We drove my truck up, figuring it'd give us more room than Eli's charger. Lottie takes the passenger seat, leaving Eli in the back.

The ride to the bar is short, only about twenty minutes through town, and we spend it bumping to early 2000's throwbacks. Nothing beats the classics.

Nelly Furtado's " Promiscuous Girl" is blasting through the speakers when we pull up to the bar.

The bar is absolutely packed, people lingering out front, and no room to park in the lot. We circle around the block, finally finding a spot two streets over.

We walk hand in hand with Lottie, taking up either side to keep her away from the traffic on the busy street.

"We'll try to find a spot that's not too crowded, but just let us know if it's too much, we can always head back to the hotel." He assures her, surely remembering her initial reaction to Myth.

She nods tightly, always retreating back into silence when she's uncomfortable. I've learned not to let it bother me; the best option is to just let her warm up to whatever we're doing. She'll come out of her shell when she's ready.

Inside the bar, there's a stage straight to the back, hosting a live band spouting some emo, punk music. Either side of the room has a bar running the full length. A dance floor dominates the middle of the space, with only a few high tops lingering around the edge. The far corner in the back has a pool table and some dart boards that look like they've seen better days.

Eli slaps my shoulder, nodding to the upper level of the bar, which is much less crowded. We beeline straight for the stairs and head up with no issues.

We keep Lottie sandwiched between us, doing our best not to touch her while also making sure no one else bumps into her.

I'm proud of how well she seems to be doing. I know the noise probably isn't her favorite, and the flashing lights are annoying even to me, but she isn't freaking out like last time.

There's hardly anyone on the upper level, not surprising since there's no bar up here. But there are more high-tops scattered around the railings, giving us a perfect view of the bar below.

"I'll go grab us some drinks." Eli waits until Lottie is settled in a seat, quickly heading back down to the bar.

She scans the bar, looking from corner to corner at all the drunk college kids, falling all over each other, grinding on the dance floor. Her eyes find the band in the middle of a particularly loud, screaming chorus.

Her face crumples, disgust written all over it.

"I take it you won't be looking to download their playlist?" I joke.

She cuts her eyes to me, shaking her head.

"T-they're so loud." She comments, "W-what are they even s-saying?"

I listen to the jumbled mess of words, trying to make sense of them.

"Something, something, Devil eyes, something, something, cry?" We both freeze, immediately falling into a fit of laughter at the ridiculousness of it.

Eli appears, drinks in hand, setting them out on the table for us. Two beers and, of course, a fruity cocktail for our girl.

She doesn't waste any time, immediately grabbing it and chugging half the glass in a single pass.

"I knew I should have gotten two," He says, eyeing the glass.

"I'll get next round. Just remember, we have all night, and you're a bit of a lightweight." I poke her side, making her jump. But she finally releases the death grip on the glass, taking a break.

As the night carries on, the music only gets worse, but for some reason, the crowd seems to love it. Lottie goes from sober and tense to officially tipsy and relaxed, her legs tossed over my lap while she reclines into Eli's chest. His fingers are running through her hair aimlessly while she points out different people she sees in the crowd. One person with blue hair, one with tattoos up to his neck, one with a full standing mohawk. She notices the smallest things that I would usually overlook, but hearing her commentary is making my night.

"Maybe I should dye my hair?" She muses.

"No."

"Not a chance."

Eli and I speak in unison, thankfully in agreement.

Her glassy eyes narrow at me, "Why not?"

"It's *brown*. Brown hair is boring." She slurs, suddenly alert, she adds, "Maybe that's why *I'm* boring." She nods to herself, like she just solved some great mystery.

"You, Lottie-girl, are the furthest thing from boring," I assure her, squeezing her thigh.

Eli gathers her hair over one shoulder, exposing the curve of her neck. His lips brush featherlight kisses along her skin, making goosebumps break out over her legs.

"I think your brown hair is hot." He murmurs, sealing his lips over her pulse point. Her eyes roll back before slipping shut, her lips part, and I can just make out the moan that falls from her lips.

The room seems to tighten around me, heat creeping up my spine as I shift in my seat, trying- and failing- to ignore the growing pressure in my jeans.

“Why don’t we call it a night?” I suggest clearing my throat.

They both agree, we help Lottie up slowly, steadying her once she's on her feet.

Eli seems sober enough, but I make sure to keep a hand on her arm down the stairs, not wanting her to lose her footing and slip.

The night air is crisp the second we step outside, a relieving contrast from the heat inside the bar.

Lottie stands on the sidewalk, swaying slightly with her flushed face upturned towards the night sky.

Ushering her between us again, we start the walk towards the car. She’s doing her best, but it seems the alcohol has slowed her down, her feet dragging on the pavement.

Eli stops her, crouching down in front of her. “Hop on.”

“Seriously?” She doesn’t even wait for him to respond, wrapping her arms around his neck and climbing onto his back.

“Jesus,” I mutter when the position causes her dress to ride up, flashing me her lacy black panties. I step forward, shielding her from flashing anyone else on the street.

"It's fine," Eli calls over his shoulder, heading towards the car.

"Just don't drop her," I warn, focusing on not stepping on his heels.

"Yes, *Dad*." He mocks, making her fall into a fit of laughter, her head tipping back and hair slapping me in the face, where it cascades down her back. My hands shoot forward, ready to catch her if she slips, but she steadies herself, resting her cheek on his shoulder.

We make it to the car without any injuries, opening the door for him, I stand by while he deposits her into the front seat, pulling her seatbelt over her as she studies him with hooded eyes.

Shutting the door, I pray for strength as I round the car, willing my dick to get the memo that now is *not* the time.

Our 2000's throwbacks are replaced on the ride back by Lottie's Taylor Swift playlist. And her usual gentle humming is replaced by very loud, very off-key singing. I think she even manages to get some of the lyrics right here and there.

I catch Eli in the rearview, staring at her with a dumb smile he can't wipe off his face. He can't tear his eyes away from her, playing with his snakebites, he looks at her like she hung the moon.

He offers her another piggyback ride when we get back to the hotel, which I swiftly decline for her, not wanting the entire lobby to catch a glimpse of all she was showing off earlier.

She doesn't even look twice at her computer when we get to the room, bypassing it completely to fall into the corner of the couch, letting out a rush of air as she sinks into the cushions.

Kicking off her shoes, she tucks her feet under her, dropping her head back.

"I think I needed that." She announces to no one in particular.

We each take a seat on either side of her, enjoying the silence and being off our feet.

"Do you want another drink?" Eli offers, "I can make you something."

"Nah, I think I'm done drinking. I really don't want to feel another hangover again tomorrow."

Probably a smart idea, I'm sure tomorrow morning will bring us a frantic Lottie, glued to her computer to make up for any lost time tonight. Might as well enjoy her company while we have it.

"Do you want to watch a movie, or something?" I offer.

She stares at the ceiling, biting her bottom lip, looking like she's holding back whatever she wants to say.

"Or something," She whispers.

The words barely leave her mouth before she sucks in a deep breath, bracing herself.

Slowly, she pushes herself up, shifting onto her knees before closing the distance between us. One leg slips over my lap, and suddenly she's there, straddling my lap.

Her pulse pounds widely in her throat, drawing my attention as her eyes shift back to mine, bright, unsteady, and lit with something that makes my own breath stall in my lungs.

Her lip is still caught between her teeth, like she doesn't know what to do with herself.

I hold myself completely still, as any movement might shatter whatever courage she's gathering. But I also try not to draw more attention to my rapidly stiffening cock, painfully aware of every inch left between us and how little space there is to hide my body's reaction to her.

I see Eli shift in my peripheral vision, one arm over the back of the couch while he watches, silently waiting.

Her hands reach out, playing absently with the buttons on my shirt while her gaze fixes there, avoiding mine.

"Do you remember the drive-in? H-how you two-“ She trails off, unable to finish.

Eli's hand drifts closer, pushing her hair away from her face so he can see her.

“How we made you cum so hard that you passed out?” He guesses, his voice taunt, barely above a whisper.

Eyes still downcast, she nods, the movement small.

“I w-want.” Her voice catches, she swallows before trying again. “I want you to t-teach me how to do t-that.” Her eyes find mine, lingering before sliding to his, “B-both of you.”

Fuck me.

22

~ Eli ~

Holy shit.

I just about swallow my tongue, not able to believe what she just asked us.

I stare at her, trying to process what she's asking, and my mind stutters, struggling to catch up with my body.

My dick is standing at attention, ready to go like a teen going through puberty seeing porn for the first time.

One look at Kai tells me he's just as shocked as I am.

"Are you sure?" I manage to ask, needing to say something before the silence has her second-guessing herself. I know how easily she can pull herself back if she misreads our reactions.

And the last thing I want is for her to take this back.

Looking me in the eyes, she nods once, firm and decisive.

"Yes."

Her lack of stutter lets me know just how sure she is in this moment, that she truly wants this.

Kai hasn't moved an inch, in total shock over her request. It looks like I'll have to take the lead here.

Pushing myself off the couch, I drift closer to her until my chest meets her back. Feeling the slight tremble running through her, I drag my hands up to rest on her shoulders, steadying her.

"The key is to move slowly, drag every moment out and build the tension, like a wave forming in the ocean, approaching the shore." Lowering my voice to a whisper, I knead the back of her neck. "Start by running your hands over his chest. Take your time, let your hands roam."

Her shaking hands fidget with his shirt buttons while she works up the courage. Finally releasing them, she places her palms flat on his chest, sliding them up and dragging them back down towards his stomach, experimenting.

"See how his breathing is speeding up?" I ask, "That means he likes it. His mind is probably racing, wondering what you'll do next."

Dropping my face next to hers, I let my breath brush across her ear as I speak.

"He won't know your next move," I brush my lips against her shoulder, feathering kisses up the side of her neck, heading back down towards that sweet spot that drives her crazy. “That uncertainty will drive him crazy.” Lingering there, I make her wait, feeling her squirm with anticipation.

“Explore him with your mouth. Take your time, taste him, memorize the curves of his body. And when you’re ready.” I graze her with my teeth, releasing her quickly as soon as I hear her gasp. “You’ll know exactly where to land.”

I give her space, but not distance, keeping my hands on her while she continues to rake her hands over his chest, slipping them into his shirt to feel his skin under her hands.

Ever so slowly, her body leans into his, continuing her exploration while she places her lips on his neck.

His eyes fall shut, his throat working under her lips.

I watch the tension take hold of him, muscles taut, hands clenched at his side as he forces himself to stay still, to let her lead.

She switches sides, exploring every inch of skin she can get to. Without any direction, she brings her lips up to his, falling into a heated kiss.

His hands move from the couch, slipping up to grip her thighs, his fingers turning white from his grasp.

My hands slip from her shoulders, dropping down to cup her chest, building her up until she’s like putty between us.

When her hips start rocking, searching against him, I drop my hands, stopping her.

She doesn't pull away from the kiss, so I wrap a hand in her hair, using the slightest pressure to pull her back.

They're both gasping for air, flushed cheeks, and swollen lips.

Kai's eyes are glazed over, studying her while his tongue traces her lips, savoring the taste of her that lingers.

"Remember, you need to go slow." I remind her. "Now, see how worked up he looks?"

Her chest heaves, and she studies him, looking closely. I see her nod, chuckling when I have to pull her back from trying to lean into him again.

"He's absolutely crazy for you. Can you see what you do to him?" She's quick to nod this time, assessing my grip to see if I'll let her fall into him. I don't.

Releasing her hair, I cup her jaw, tilting it down so she can see the obvious reaction his body has to her.

She stops fighting my hold, freezing at the sight of it.

"You can touch," I whisper in her ear, but this time she doesn't move.

Her breathing speeds up, and I can feel her tensing, suddenly not so sure of her next move, and not able to pull herself out of her head.

“Why don’t you help her out, Kai?” I suggest giving him a chance to take the reins for a moment.

Without pulling his eyes from her, he reaches down, unbuttoning his jeans and freeing himself, not giving her any time to panic, before he takes her hand, guiding it forward. Slowly. Giving her a chance to pull away, but she doesn’t.

Finally, her hand lands on his dick, his groan drowning out the small whimper I can hear escaping her.

He lets go, letting her trail her fingers over his length, tracing the veins from the base to the tip and back down.

His head falls back against the couch, and I can see the effort it takes to restrain himself, but he holds out, letting her explore in her own time.

When I can see it’s getting to be too much for him, I step back in.

“Wrap your hand around it,” I direct her, refusing to help her as he did. I draw the line at having my hand that close to my brother’s dick.

She barely wraps her hand around it, treating it like a venomous snake that might jump up and bite her.

“You can grab it tighter than that; you won’t hurt him,” I assure her, waiting for her to fix her grip. “Now, you want to stroke it, start slow, and you can pick up the pace when you’re ready. Don’t be afraid to grab him tightly; it will feel good, I promise.”

The ball is in her court now, moving my hands back to her shoulders, I remain a solid presence behind her, something to ground her as she builds up courage.

She moves her hand tentatively, testing the movement and studying his face as she does. I think she's about to pull back when his face twists in discomfort on a particularly hard pull, but it morphs into pleasure on her next pass. Testing, she tries again, and she's rewarded with a low moan.

The more she moves, the faster his breath comes, unable to contain his sounds of pleasure as she begins to pick up speed.

He's rushing higher, approaching the edge when he drops his head to his chest, cursing when he sees her hand wrapped around him.

"Fuuuuck."

Without warning, he cums, coating her hand while she watches, fascinated with the way his body jerks, twitching as he comes back down to Earth.

I don't have to tell her to stop; her movements slow as his panting breaths begin to go back to normal, only pulling away when he's fully relaxed.

We both watch, in total fascination, as she holds her hand up, examining it closely before bringing it to her mouth, her tongue darting out to lick some of it up, tasting it.

"Oh, shit. Lottie, that was amazing, but if you sit here and lick my cum off your fingers, I'm going to die."

I can't help but laugh, between his tortured face and the look of pure innocence on hers.

His narrowed eyes find mine.

"Oh, you think it's funny? Alright, your turn, *brother*."

Shit.

23

~ Charlotte ~

I don't even have time to understand what just happened. My mind is in a daze, I can't gather my thoughts, and with Eli telling me what to do, I was able to just shut off my brain. Not having to think about the next step made it impossibly easy to slowly torture Kai, and watching him unravel has me on the edge myself.

I can't stop my hips from shifting against his lap, searching for some friction to ease the ache building inside me.

"Oh no," Kai stops me with his hands on my waist, "Save that for Eli, Lottie-girl. He helped you help me, now it's my turn." He shoots me a devilish wink, easing me off his lap.

Turning me to face him, Eli catches my eyes with his.

"Only if you want to, we can stop." The idea of stopping now makes me more anxious than continuing, knowing that I'll be left wondering what might've happened or what it would've been like.

"I'm okay," I assure him, earning a kiss on the forehead as he takes Kai's vacant spot on the couch.

"Go ahead and show him what you learned." Kai urges, leading me by my shoulders, he guides me over Eli's lap.

I don't let my mind wander, focusing solely on my hands on his chest, tracing lines with my fingertips.

I know Eli told me to move slowly, to really build the tension, but I'm getting impatient after dragging it out so long with Kai. And judging by the stiffening member I can feel brushing my thigh, I think he's been teasing himself this whole time already.

I go straight for a kiss, savoring the taste of him and relishing the way his snakebite piercings are cool to the touch on my heated skin.

Again, when I try to move closer, I'm stopped.

Kai's hands locking down on my hips to keep me from finding any of my own pleasure. Something sounding like a growl mixed with a mewl slips out of my throat, causing him to laugh.

"Easy," He murmurs. "We'll take care of you."

His hand fists my hair, pulling my face towards him. Closing the space slowly, my breath hitches, and I think he's going to go in for another kiss, but he skims his lips over my cheek until his breath ghosts against my ear.

"Do you want to keep going?"

I nod as much as his hand in my hair will allow, instinctively chasing him when he pulls back.

He pulls me off of Eli's lap, steadying me on my feet before jutting his chin towards him, silently issuing his demands.

Eli must understand enough to shift to free himself from his jeans, much like Kai did.

I wouldn't have ever guessed that seeing the male appendage would turn me on, but I'm proven wrong with my body's reaction to both of theirs. My mouth waters, and my thighs tighten; a fire raging inside me warms me from my core.

"Eli showed you how to tease me with your hands, which I loved, but I'm going to show you another way to drive him crazy."

He gathers my head at the nape of my neck, keeping my head directed at Eli, sitting exposed and panting, rooted in place.

"You can also get him off with your *mouth.*" His voice becomes thick, arousal evident as he palms his crotch, already hardening again.

"Shit," I hear Eli curse under his breath. Shifting his arms to lie along the back of the couch, his hands grab fistfuls of the fabric.

"W-what do I do?" I need the direction, never having done this. It's not something I want to screw up, but also, it seems like such an easy thing to fuck up on. It puts both of us in a very vulnerable position, which leaves a lot of room for error.

"First thing you'll want to do is get on your knees in front of him." He grabs a throw pillow, placing it between Eli's feet to provide some cushion.

"You should be able to rest your weight on your heels so your knees don't take the brunt of this. Use what he already taught you, let your hands explore while you're down there, watch his breathing, his reactions. Those will tell you how much he's loving this."

Nervous anticipation builds in my stomach. I want to do this for him, and I don't want to panic and stop now, not when I'm learning so much, and I know I'm making them feel good.

It makes me feel powerful. Desirable.

I drop down onto the throw pillow, a bit too roughly, feeling the sting in my knees.

Eli shifts, ready to catch me, but I feel Kai's hands on my shoulders, keeping me upright as I steady myself with my hands on Eli's thighs.

I can feel the warmth of his skin through my fingers. He's burning hotter than the fire rushing through my veins.

That oddly makes me feel better.

To know I'm not the only one feeling affected.

Pushing everything out of my brain except the instructions Kai gave me, I let my hands wander.

I feel his soft skin and the hard contours of his stomach muscles as they flex under my hands. I feel the contrast between the rough skin of his thighs and the smooth, silky skin on his abdomen and up onto his chest.

He stays perfectly still while I pull the edges of his shirt apart, giving me a complete view of his entire chest.

Something catches my eye: he has two metal bars stuck through each of his nipples, matching the color of the piercings under his lips.

Curious, I touch them. Watching, mesmerized at the way I can twist them, rolling them under his skin.

His chest jumps, sucking in a deep breath, and his head falls back. His Adam's apple bobs as his throat works and his hands ball into fists.

A sudden urge to taste them, to see what they'd feel like under my tongue strikes, but I heed Kai's instructions and continue to run my hands over his body.

My hair is pulled off my shoulders.

Kai's breath brushes my ear as he leans down.

"You're doing great, Lottie-girl." His lips brush my neck, teasing but not lingering, making my own breathing speed up, matching Eli's.

"You've got him all worked up. Look at his face."

My eyes lift, taking in Eli's pained expression. Eyes squeezed shut, and his jaw clenched. I can see him grinding his teeth, his jaw working back and forth.

"Now, the same thing you did with your hands earlier to me, do that with your mouth. Taste him, explore him, do whatever feels right."

Shifting my focus back to Eli's dick, standing at full attention, looking painful the way it's pulsing.

I see a drop of something clear and shiny on the tip. Without giving it much thought, I lean forward, sticking my tongue out to taste it.

A salty flavor explodes on my tongue, similar to when I licked my hand.

It's oddly addicting.

Using my tongue this time, I trace the veins up his shaft, following them down to the base and along the underside back up to the tip, collecting more of the salty substance.

I feel Kai's hand thread into my hair again. Guiding me this time.

With light pressure, he eases my head forward until I have no choice but to open my mouth, accepting Eli's length.

Instinctively, my lips seal around him as I feel him gliding across my tongue.

His skin feels like glass as I continue forward, easing my way to the base.

As I move further, I can feel the tip tickling the back of my throat, causing me to gag.

My body jerks, and I rush to pull back.

Kai's hand keeps me still, but he lets me pull back enough to the tip.

"Good, girl. Just like that." He croons, encouraging me and keeping my panic at bay for the moment.

He lets me take a couple of slow passes, testing my limits and getting more confident with each one.

"When you get to the tip, try swirling your tongue around the top. Seal your lips around him to give him that pressure and think about stroking him with your tongue. Breathe through your nose, it might be hard, but you're okay, you can breathe."

Listening to him, I try it.

Sucking with my lips, my tongue strokes along the bottom. Getting back to the top, I swirl my tongue, rewarded with the salty taste.

Each time I reach the tip and taste the salty flavor, I get even more eager.

My speed increases without thought.

Kai takes one of my hands from Eli's thigh, moving it towards the base of his dick. Without any prompting, I grab it, applying pressure as I did with Kai, my mouth still working.

An ache starts to form in my jaw, but I ignore it. All I can focus on is the taste of him and the sound of his breathing, morphing into gasping breaths while his body starts to twitch.

"Shit, I'm right there." Eli's voice comes out raspy and choked.

Kai's hand leaves my hair. Seconds later, I feel it skim my thigh, making me jump when I feel him inch it upwards towards my aching core.

I can't even argue before I feel his fingers right where I need him. Slippery from my own essence, they land right on that bundle of nerves. Applying pressure, he offers that friction I've been looking for, sending sparks through every nerve ending in my body.

My pace falters. My brain struggling to keep up with all the added sensations from Kai's hands.

"Don't stop." He growls in my ear, biting my earlobe in the process, only adding to it. "He's so close, and so are you. Do you feel the way your body is shaking, begging for release? So is his. Keep going, and you'll both get to finish."

His words are the encouragement I need.

Doubling down, I throw all of my focus into helping Eli. Relishing the tremble in his thighs as he gets closer and closer.

My hips buck wildly, meeting Kai's fingers and taking what I need from him, driving myself higher and higher.

"I'm going to- fuck, I can't-shit." Eli's words become a jumbled mess, not making any sense.

“If you don’t want to swallow, then pull back and use your hand. Now.” Kai’s words are rushed, tapping me on the shoulder to get my attention. But I’m too far gone to really hear him.

I feel Eli stiffen in my mouth, seconds before his cock begins to spasm.

A rush of heat lands on my tongue, bursts of his salty cum filling my mouth.

I swallow it down, not wanting to choke.

His cock softens slightly, but still he fills my mouth as I hit a wall.

Like a freight train barreling into me, I reach that point of ecstasy.

My body is like a livewire, seizing as the pit in my stomach explodes, all the sensations washing over me.

My hips finally still, keeping the pressure on the bundle of nerves as I drag out the feeling, not wanting it to end.

Just like last time, once the feeling begins to dissipate, my body goes limp.

Sliding off of Eli's cock, I watch his body deflate as well.

Falling back, Kai's arms catch me before I can fall, letting me relax.

Silence lingers between us, the only sounds being our heavy breathing as we all take a moment.

"Well, that was fun." Kai finally breaks the silence, earning a snort from Eli.

Eli tucks himself back in his jeans, and Kai pulls my dress back down my thighs before lifting me in his arms, setting me back on the couch, and sitting on my other side.

"Did I do okay?" I have to ask them both.

It felt amazing to me, but I still need the confirmation. To know that I'm not just lost in my own pleasure.

Eli's hands cup my face, dragging me towards him for another suffocating kiss.

"That was so fucking amazing, Charlie." Kissing me once more, he pulls back. "You're amazing."

Passing me off to Kai, he follows suit.

Dominating the kiss and making me feel like I'm drowning, struggling to come up for air.

"What he said." Is his simple response.

I can't help the stupid smile plastered to my face. Feeling thoroughly accomplished that I was able to do something for both of them.

These men do everything for me, and having the power to offer them something, to make them feel good for once, it's a rush.

Since I've gotten out of the hospital, I've had a tiny voice in the back of my head, always telling me that they think

I'm broken. They always treat me like I'm made of glass. But tonight, it didn't feel like they saw me that way.

Tonight, it feels like they see me as more.

24

~ Charlotte ~

As much fun as our night out was, there hasn't been much more fun since then.

The next morning, we were right back in the thick of things, working to find any angle to work against Beck if Maverick managed to get a questioning set up with him.

It's been almost a week of being holed up in the hotel room, Eli and I working around the clock to find anything we could.

I was still working on tracing the dark web listing, refusing to give up on it because I know it will open a lot of doors for us. If I could just figure it out.

Eli was working on finding an entry point to any of the devices registered at the bar. So far, he's only managed to get into their POS system, which was progress, but it didn't help us with the case. He's been struggling for days, having found two personal computers that he just couldn't get into, no matter what he tried.

Kai had taken to going to the bar every night. After we finally found Beck on the feeds, he wanted to be there, close in case he made any attempts to grab another girl.

I think being stuck inside all day was starting to get to him. And as much as he has a good reason to stake out the bar, it was just as much for his mental state as it was for the case.

Cooper called to check in yesterday, letting us know that they don't have any word from the sheriff yet, but that they thought he might be getting close to setting us up with the local police force here.

That's another thing I've had to check in addition to the listing. I've been trying to run checks on all the cops on their payroll, looking for any indication that they might be working under the table with Beck, which would explain why the cases are being closed so easily.

It's just after four in the morning, my eyes are gritty, and I'm barely managing to keep them open.

I don't think I've slept in over a day now, maybe two? I was starting to lose it, and my energy drinks weren't really helping me stay afloat anymore.

The door clicks shut, alerting me to Kai's arrival.

He tiptoes into the room, probably hoping that Eli and I have finally passed out from exhaustion.

He's been on edge a lot, trying to force both of us to sleep on top of making sure we're both taking breaks to eat and shower, at least.

He gives up his quiet act once he sees us both awake. Bringing over a bag of fast food, distributing it to both of us.

We all take a spot on the couch, thankful for the break, digging into the food.

“Any luck?” He asks through a mouthful of fries.

Eli glares at him. He hates it when Kai talks with a mouthful.

“Nothing,” I admit dejectedly. Picking at my fries, but just not having an appetite, the longer this drags out.

We stew in our silence.

My mind just won’t shut off. The more days that pass without being able to find anything, the more my thoughts drift. Taking me to darker places, imagining the worst for the girls. I feel like I’m letting them down, and whatever fate they’re suffering is in my hands the longer I can’t figure it out.

“I have an idea…” Kai offers, hesitating.

Immediately, I’m on edge, wondering what he possibly came up with.

“Well?” Eli snaps impatiently when he doesn’t continue.

Setting his food to the side, Kai takes a breath. Steadying himself.

“When I was at the bar tonight, nothing looked out of the ordinary. Beck was there, but he was mostly in his office.

I stayed until last call, and he left right before they locked up for the night, and I noticed something." He pauses again, his leg bouncing.

"And?" Eli urges, "Spit it out already."

"And I watched him walk out of his office. He didn't stop to lock it like I've seen every other night he's been there."

I'm lost, not getting his point.

"Okay?" I don't know what else to say. It's a good observation, but I can't see how it helps us.

"I've also been watching the feeds for a couple of hours every morning when I get back here, while you two are lost in your own computers." He gestures to the workstations we have set up.

I try to recall him watching the feeds, but come up with nothing. I figured he was gaming or streaming shows when he got back before crashing each morning.

"They call for last call, clean the bar, and lock up. Every day. No one else shows up at the bar until later in the afternoon to set up for the next shift."

"No," Eli says, startling me. "I know what you're thinking, and the answer is no. It's too risky."

"It's a good idea!" Kai argues. "It'd be quick, and no one is there, and you have access to the cameras."

"What's a good idea?" I finally ask. They both are obviously on the same page, but I feel like I'm in a different book. No clue what they're talking about.

"It's a *horrible* idea." Eli reiterates, looking at me. He adds, "He wants to break into the bar and look at Beck's computer."

My initial reaction is right on par with Eli's. Thinking it's a bad idea. We could get caught; anything we find, we wouldn't be able to use against Beck because of how we found it. Did I mention we could get caught?

But then again, being able to check things directly on Beck's computer would mean I could find evidence that he accessed Ivy's listing. Or I could find out if he was the one who posted it. I could look into his entire history, even if he thinks he's deleted it. I can check everything. This would let me see whether we were even on the right track or chasing a dead lead.

"It's not the worst idea," I admit, keeping my voice low, seeing how upset Eli already is.

He throws his head back, dragging his hands through his hair, gripping it at the roots.

"You've got to be kidding me."

"I-I'm not s-saying it's the smartest idea." I amend.

"B-but we've been spending so much time looking, without finding a-anything."

"So we keep looking, we don't need to break in and hack his computer. What if he comes back?" He asks.

"He doesn't ever come back until later in the night," Kai argues. "I can stay out front, looking out for anyone. You can access the cameras and wipe them so no one can see we were there, and Lottie can go in, check his computer, and be out before you know it."

I don't want to pit them against each other, but I have to agree with Kai. It sounds simple enough. And it would pay off in the end.

"I don't e-even have to check e-everything there." I offer. "I c-can offload his computer to m-mine. Then we can check it out h-here."

Holding my breath, I wait. Hoping that he can see this is the best option for us right now.

I know he's caved when he falls back into the couch. Sighing with defeat.

"I'll give you ten minutes inside. After that, I'm dragging you back out. We can't block the feeds for any longer than that, or it will be obvious that they were tampered with." He relents.

I shouldn't even need that long, but I'm thankful that he's going along with this.

"We'll head out in an hour. It should still be pretty quiet, fewer witnesses, and everyone will be cleared out by then." Kai decides, grabbing his food and retreating to his room.

Eli stews silently, picking at his burger wrapper.

"Do you really think this is a good idea?" He asks suddenly.

I think it over, trying to find any alternative we might have. But I come up empty. It's taking longer than we thought to get the warrant for Beck to question him, and even if we do get a chance to, there's no guarantee that he'll say anything of any use to us. And then we'll be right back to square one with nothing.

"I think it's the only choice we have right now," I admit.

"I meant what I said, you get in and get out. I don't care if you don't find anything. I'm not letting you stay in there to get caught." He reminds me.

"I know." I agree. I can see the tension in his face. He doesn't like this plan at all, but he's doing it for me. Because he knows how much I've put into this, how much I want to find the girls.

"Maverick's going to be pissed." He comments.

That's an understatement if I've ever heard one. Maverick is going to lose his mind, but if we can find something, then hopefully that will soften the blow.

"Then we'd better make sure it's worth it."

25

~ Kai ~

Maybe this was a bad idea.

That's the only thing I can think of, watching Lottie slip into the back door of the bar while Eli hops back into the car.

He made sure to disable their alarm system from his laptop before picking the lock for her.

So far, so good. She's made it inside without setting anything off.

Eli has eyes on her, his laptop glued to his lap, while I round the front of the building, heading to a gas station across the street so we can still keep watch without drawing any attention to ourselves.

Someone might question a random car parked out front while the bar's closed.

The streets are empty, still too early for most to be out yet. The only people we see are all the blue-collar workers filtering in and out of the gas station for their morning pit stops.

I lean over, watching over Eli's shoulder at the live footage on the screen. We can see Charlotte moving through the bar in one window, another holds a line of code that Eli explained was the coding window he was using to wipe the footage as she went.

Seeing her on the screen, sneaking around made this significantly more real. And the risks associated were all I could think of, playing in my mind on repeat as the minutes ticked by.

She disappears from the camera's view, slipping into the back hallway that leads to the offices.

I had her call me while wearing her AirPods so she could be hands-free. Through my phone, we can hear her entering the office, setting down her laptop, and keys clicking as she gets to work.

"What the hell?" I hear her whisper.

"What? What happened?" I'm on high alert, already reaching to put the car in drive to go get her.

"Nothing," She assures me quickly. "There's just a picture in his office." Her voice trails off.

"Of what?"

"Timothy."

Who the fuck is Timothy?

Looking to Eli for clarification, Eli has his brows scrunched up.

"That kid who slashed my tires?" He asks.

"Yeah," At least she sounds just as confused as I feel.

Why the fuck would Beck have a photo with a high school student from Jacksonville?

"We'll look into it later, just hurry up." Eli tells her, "You have five minutes."

I roll my eyes. He sounds more like Maverick than he'd ever admit. But I keep that to myself; being in close quarters like this isn't the time to point that out.

"I'm almost done," She assures him.

My little hacker.

As nervous as I am, I can't help but beam with pride. She's such a badass right now.

Breaking and entering, stealing this jackass's computer…stuff. She's so hot.

She was nervous the whole way here, fidgeting with her hands, silently staring out the window. Her anxiety was palpable. But still, here she is, taking what she needs to shut this shit down.

"Done." She calls over the phone, springing Eli and me into action.

Throwing the car in drive, I sail back across the street, rounding to the back door of the bar while Eli taps away at the screen.

"Remember to shut his door," He reminds her, "And flip the lock on the back door when you come out.

He's so busy, tapping away on the keyboard, that he isn't watching her slip out of the back of the bar.

"Charlie?" He barks when she doesn't reply.

He jumps out of his seat when she slides into the back seat, setting her computer aside and buckling in.

"Done, and done." She smiles widely at him, ignoring his narrowed eyes.

I only ever see her sass thrown towards Mav; it's a refreshing change of pace to see it directed at someone else. And after the stressful couple of days of non-stop searching, it's good to see a playful side of her coming out.

We head back to the hotel, successfully undetected in our mission to break into the bar.

Eli works the whole way there, making sure all the cameras are wiped and that no one will be able to tell if they check them.

Lottie is significantly more relaxed on the drive back, humming quietly along with the radio and watching over Eli's shoulder.

She wastes no time once we're back, rushing through the lobby with a death grip on her laptop, fidgeting the whole ride up the elevator, darting out the doors as soon as they open.

Inside the room, she beelines straight for her desk, plugging her computer and bringing the screens to life.

Countless windows are open, everything that she's been working on for the last few days.

She minimizes those, pulling a new one up on the full screen so we can see. A new desktop appears after a few moments, featuring multiple icons and a backdrop of a busty supermodel perched on a Harley in a string bikini.

"Classy," Eli laughs.

It's cheesy for sure, and fits the persona I've made up in my mind of Beck.

She shifts into another mindset as she starts looking through everything. Any playfulness from the car is long gone as she's locked in.

Eli and I hover on either side of her, watching over her shoulders, and after a few minutes, she pushes her chair back. I have to jump out of the way to avoid her bumping into me.

"Okay, I know you two want to help, but I can't focus with you watching over me."

Raising my hands up, I step back.

"My bad," I apologize. Heading for the couch to get out of her way.

Eli rubs a hand over the back of his neck.

“I’ll just, uh, get back to work.” He murmurs, stepping over to his computer.

We let her work for a couple of hours, Eli stays at his computer, and I channel surf the TV, officially out of things to do to be helpful.

When the afternoon rolls around, I head out to grab food, bring it back, and make sure they both eat, which proves to be a challenge with Lottie. She’s so invested in the computer that I can barely tear her away to inhale a couple of bites at least.

I must fall asleep sometime after dinner, because the next thing I know, I’m waking up on the couch to the sound of Eli talking quietly on his phone beside me, morning light streaming through the windows.

“Alright, sounds good. We’ll see you then.”

Stretching out, I feel my neck crack. Sitting up, I wait for him to end the call.

“Who was that?” I ask.

“Mav,” Pocketing his phone, he glances back at Lottie, still behind her computer, paying us no attention.

“They finally got a warrant to bring Beck in for questioning.” He tells me, “He and Cooper will be here on Friday.”

Stealing a glance at Lottie myself, I worry that telling her is going to cause a spiral. She hasn’t stopped digging into his computer, looking for anything. If we tell her we only have two days before meeting Beck face-to-face, she might lose it. Knowing that we have to rely on him saying something to incriminate himself, and right now, that's not a bet I'd take.

"Do you think she'll be able to find something in two days?" I wonder, hoping he's more optimistic than I feel.

"We can only hope."

Fuck.

That was not the reassurance I was hoping for.

26

~ Charlotte ~

Fuck Beckett Fisher.

That's all I have to say about this guy.

I've had no sleep. I'm running on empty. And I still haven't found anything on his stupid computer.

To top it all off, I'm not on a time crunch.

Kai finally told me last night that Maverick and Cooper were on their way and they'd be here tomorrow. It's good because we're finally going to get to question Beck, but if he doesn't say anything we can hold against him, then we have nothing left to work off of.

There's just so much shit to sort through on this damn computer.

This guy has his entire life on here; it's like he's only ever owned this one device, and he's used it for every simple task since.

He still has book reports from high school saved on here, for God's sake. The man is in his late twenties.

Unsurprisingly, everything on here is also password-protected. So that adds another layer of tedious, time-wasting tasks just to view every file.

Eli and Kai are both out. They needed to restock on some essentials and wanted to grab a couple more sets of clothes since they've been taking ours down to the hotel laundromat every couple of days.

I'm trying to get as much done as I can while they're out, taking advantage of the peace and quiet.

It's not that they've been in my way; they've actually tried to keep a wide berth to let me work. It's just even when they're trying to give me space, I can still feel them hovering. They're constantly waiting for me to call out for help or to remind me to eat and take a break.

This far into all of this crap, I don't need a break. I just need answers.

I don't know how much time has passed when they get back to the hotel, walking through the door with shopping bags in hand.

"Hey, Lottie." Kai places a kiss on my head, his hands on my shoulders, kneading the knots that are permanently stuck in my neck.

"Still nothing?" Eli asks, sending a spark of anger through me.

I know he means well, but I'm tired of being asked the same thing every day. And not having a new answer.

"Why don't you take a break?" Kai insists quietly.

I shake my head, quickly shutting him down.

"Not right now."

"Lottie," He sighs, ready for a fight. But I don't have the time.

"I have three more files to check, and my software should be almost done sorting through his search history. I can't take a break right now, just please let me finish this." It takes all my effort to keep my voice level, and by some miracle, I keep the stutter from my voice.

It must be enough for him to think I'm calm enough to rationalize this, because he agrees quickly, leaving me to work while they unpack their purchases.

I don't even make it to the next file before I get the alert that the software scanning his never-ending history is complete.

I filtered it to pull out any unusual sites from his normal usage, and I plugged in the web address from Ivy's listing to cross-match it against anything in the history.

Most of the history that it pulled for me looks to just be weird porn sites.

Gross.

There are a few that are indescribable, though.

Clicking through those, I find a few different things. One leads to a bank login page. It's not one that I recognize, and a quick search tells me it's based in Nassau. There's not much information on it, so I set it aside for later.

The next one is a site that I'm familiar with. I've even used it before. On previous freelance projects, I've needed to spoof my IP address so my computer isn't traceable when accessing business systems remotely and without detection.

Experimenting with the site, I copy the IP address from his computer, plugging it into the site to get the previous spoofs.

The list it generates is only about ten different addresses. Copying those, I put them in a note and set them to the side.

The last site is nothing more than a web-based phone service. No matter how much I dig around, I can't see his previous calls made from the site, so I close that one out, writing it off as a waste.

With something more tangible now, I dig up the log I saved with IP's associated with the listing.

It took me two weeks, back when I started this, to find out how to see the sources of the post about Ivy on the dark web.

But since I have it, I compare the spoofed IPs with the log I have saved.

Bingo.

His IP is not only on the list but has interacted with the listing since it went up. One of the spoofed IPs is also at the top of the list, being named the source.

Dropping back in my chair, I stare in disbelief.

Weeks of searching, and now we *finally* have something.

"Charlie?" Eli's voice makes me jump. Standing beside me, he looks down, concern heavy in his eyes.

"I found it." My voice is only a whisper, like speaking too loudly will make it all disappear.

"What?" His voice is much louder, borderline yelling. Darting forward, he stares at the screen, his face mere inches from it as he reads.

"Holy shit! Charlie, you did it!"

Dragging me by the hand, he lifts me from the chair. Picking me up in his arms, he spins me around, making me laugh for the first time in days.

"What's going on?" Kai emerges from his room, taking in the sight of us.

Eli sets me down, "Charlie just found proof that Back is the one who put up the listing of Ivy!"

"No way!" I'm back in the air, this time in Kai's arms, spinning around.

"I knew you would find it." He smiles warmly at me, dropping down for a kiss.

“Is this something that we can use tomorrow when we talk to him?” He asks, looking between Eli and me.

“Not technically,” Eli tells him, and I watch Kai deflate like a balloon, all the excitement zapped immediately. “Since we obtained the information in a way that’s not really legal, we can’t use it without admitting guilt on our part.”

“So what can we do with it?”

“I can still look to see if there’s another way to link it to him, without using anything I found on the computer.” I offer, trying to come up with another plan in case it backfires tomorrow.

“And once we tell Mav, we can make sure that when he questions him, he really puts the pressure on. Knowing we have this in our back pocket, we can be a lot more forward with Beck and try to force a confession from him.” Eli adds.

Kai nods, “If anyone can get him to slip up, it’d be Mav. He’ll sit in that room all day until he gives us something.”

“Once there’s any suspicion on him, we can get a warrant signed off for his computer. And then we’ll already have the evidence that we need.”

“Oh shit, okay. Should we celebrate?” Kai looks to me, but I’m already swaying on my feet, the exhaustion finally dragging me under now that the adrenaline is dissipating.

"We could celebrate with sleep so that we're ready to go tomorrow?" He corrects, eyeing me carefully.

I eagerly agree, kissing them both and retreating to my room. For the first time since we got here, I collapse into the queen-sized bed, not even bothering to pull back the covers.

I'll take the small victory for today.

But I know tomorrow is only going to open up a whole new set of challenges for us.

This is just the start.

27

~ Charlotte ~

I only manage to get about five hours of sleep. Waking up around four in the morning, but luckily feeling more rested than I have in weeks.

I should probably try to get some more sleep, but now that I'm awake, my mind is running, wondering if there's anything else that I missed on Beck's computer.

I give myself time to take a shower and feel more human, even heating up a pack of noodles now that I feel like I have an appetite again, before sitting down at the computer.

The room is quiet, Eli and Kai are still both in their rooms, and I'm sure they'll sleep for a few more hours.

I take stock of the room before I start to work, noticing how cluttered it is.

Five more minutes won't kill me, so I work around the room, cleaning up trash, folding clothes, and straightening both mine and Eli's desks up until everything is back in place.

Feeling much better, I start up the computer, ready to look at it with a fresh mind.

There's not much of the computer that I haven't looked into already. Most of it was crap, and I've spent days wading through that.

The sun is shining through the windows now, and a glance at the clock tells me I've been aimlessly looking for a couple of hours.

I'm just about to close it out and see if there's anything else I can get started on when something catches my eye.

An email profile from his search history that I didn't notice yesterday.

His credentials are saved, allowing me to log in with ease to a list of outgoing emails.

Most of them are useless, looking like conversations with friends or typical marketing emails.

When I click on the saved folder, I find more interesting emails.

They look to be written discreetly, discussing 'products' being exchanged and when to meet up for 'exchanges' as well as discussing payments being behind or met.

The next email makes my blood run cold.

The subject line is 'upcoming product'. There's no text in the body of the email, only photo attachments. The first one I click on is a photo taken with a cell phone camera.

The photo is of me.

Snapped from yards away, I see myself standing outside a storefront in the mall back at home.

I remember the day, not long ago at all. We went to shop for Christmas presents, and we decided to split up. I had been outside of one of the stores when I felt like someone was watching me.

Clicking on the next photo, I see myself again. This time on the walking trail outside of my dorm, Christmas Eve. Just before Eli came to pick me up.

The last photo is from just a couple of nights ago. Taken from inside the bar, I see myself laid out, reclining against Eli with my feet in Kai's lap. It was right before we left for the night.

I feel my stomach roll. Rushing to my bathroom, I make it seconds before my stomach revolts, bringing up the noodles I ate this morning until I'm dry heaving over the bowl.

Why would he have pictures of me?

How did he get pictures of me?

What does this all mean for me now? Do I need to get the hell away from here and as far away from Beck before I end up just like Ivy?

If he's been taking girls from his bar that look easy to grab, then why would he have anything on me?

My hands shake, and I lean back against the wall, unable to hold myself up.

I try to think of any possible explanation as to how I even got on Beck's radar.

This whole time I've been looking into him, all while he's been keeping tabs on me.

Before I met the guys, I hardly left my room. I'm not sure how, in the span of a few weeks, I went from invisible to a target for a kidnapper.

Leaving here would probably be smart, putting as much distance between myself and this creep. But the photos I found pop up in my mind, reminding me that back home isn't any safer for me.

I don't know what to do.

My chest starts to feel tight, and my head spins.

My fingers go numb, the tingling spreading up my hands and into my arms, leaving me feeling paralyzed.

I'm having a panic attack, and I'm at least able to realize it.

Trying my usual tricks, I count to ten in my head, taking a breath with each count.

As much as I feel like I'm suffocating, I remind myself I'm dragging air into my lungs as I count. Even if I don't feel like it, I can still breathe.

Willing my hands to move, I drag one over to my thigh, pinching it as hard as I can.

I can barely feel the bite of my nails digging into my skin, and the numbness starts to dissipate.

Feeling my hands again, I focus on breathing, tapping my fingers to a count in my head to keep me distracted.

“Lottie?” Kai’s voice calls out from my room, seconds before he steps into the doorway of the bathroom.

Rushing over, he crouches down in front of me, his hands on either side of my face, while he checks me over.

“Did you get sick? You feel warm, do you feel okay?”

Nodding, I don’t really answer either of his questions.

His hands disappear, leaving me feeling cold. I hear him stepping around the bathroom, flushing my vomit, and the faucet running.

My eyes spring open when I feel his arms lifting me from the floor, carrying me into the bedroom.

He sits me on the bed, pulling the covers back and tucking me beneath them, and then places a cool washcloth on my forehead.

He sits beside me, running his fingers through my hair silently.

I let my eyes fall shut, focusing only on the feeling of his fingers on my scalp, hoping that will help clear my mind.

I'm on the edge of sleep when I hear footsteps, followed by Eli's voice.

"Is she okay?" His voice sounds distant, but I'm on the edge of being asleep, not able to open my eyes.

"I found her in the bathroom; she was sick," Kai tells her, shifting beside me. "I think she fell asleep."

I feel the bed shift, Kai slipping off to head towards the door.

"I think she just worked herself sick; she needs to rest." His voice trails off, and the door clicks shut as I slip further and further into the darkness.

28

~ Charlotte ~

Something cool touches my face, dragging me out of sleep.

Shooting out of the bed, I take a look around, finding Maverick on one side of me, and Cooper on the other, holding another wet washcloth.

"Hey, babe. How you feeling?" Cooper smiles.

"I told you not to wake her," Maverick growls, shooting daggers at him.

"It's fine," I reassure him, shifting back to rest against the headboard.

"We leave you for a week, and you work yourself sick. That's not fine." Maverick retorts. He hates the word fine, and I'm close to telling him I'm just that to annoy him, but I can't bring myself to say it. Knowing it would be a lie.

I should tell them what I found this morning, but they would freak out. They'd drag me back home and lock me away, afraid of what could happen.

While that might be what's best, we still have answers we need to find, and they need to talk to Beck. Otherwise, everything we've done so far is for nothing.

The thought of that is almost harder to swallow than knowing I'm at risk.

"We need to head out soon to get to the station," Maverick tells me. "You're staying here."

It's not a question, it's a statement.

One that I can't even argue with.

I don't want to be anywhere near Beck, knowing what I know.

And it's not like I feel up to it at the moment either.

"One of us can stay here with you?" Cooper offers.

"I-I'm fine. Y-you all s-should go."

Kai and Eli have been working with me and know all of the information that I've found. I need them all to try and get Beck to slip up.

And I need more time to process what my next move should be, and how I'm going to break the news to all of them if they can't get anything from Beck.

"Well, we'll have our phones on us, just call if you need anything." Leaning forward for a kiss, he heads out of the room.

Maverick reaches over to the nightstand, grabbing a bottle of water and two little pills.

"Take these, and drink." He demands, and I don't try to fight him. Not having the fight in me right now.

I swallow the pills and down half the water in one go, setting it on the nightstand beside me.

He doesn't make any move to leave. Studying me, as if he can see right through me and can see everything I'm hiding, makes me squirm.

His hand cups the back of my neck, dragging me towards him.

His eyes study mine, dropping to my lips and back again.

Brushing his lips against mine, my body sways towards him, wanting more.

He doesn't deny me, crushing his lips with mine. Our tongues war with one another, fighting for dominance of the kiss. Ultimately, he wins, biting my lips, making my thighs clench as heat blooms in my belly.

All too soon, he's pulling back. Leaning his forehead against mine.

"I missed you," He confesses, giving me one last kiss before sliding off the bed.

He helps me pull the blankets back up, letting me get settled.

"Drink your water and sleep. We'll be back later."

My eyelids become heavy as he walks away. Before he's even made it out the door, they fall shut, shutting the outside world away for a little bit longer.

***

Something drags me from the depths of sleep yet again.

My body feels stiff, and I struggle to open my eyes, still groggy and wanting to slip back into sleep.

I begin to doze off when I hear footsteps in the living room.

Figuring it's the guys coming back, I roll over. Stretching out my arms and legs to ease the stiffness.

I'm halfway asleep when the door opens.

Silence falls over the room while I wait to see who it is.

The bed dips behind me; whichever one of them it is, they must be trying not to wake me.

My hair is swept back off my neck, sending a shiver down my spine.

I feel a sharp sting on the side of my neck.

Hissing at the bite of pain, I try to open my eyes.

A cold wave rushes over me, my eyes feel like cement, sealed shut and unable to open.

“W-what?” My voice comes out slurred, my tongue feeling too big for my mouth.

I can feel my heart start to race, shaking my body with each pulse.

Even with my heart rate accelerating, I still can’t open my eyes, falling further and further away.

“Shh,” A voice sounds out behind me. “Sleep for now. You’re going to need it.”

The last thing I feel is panic overtaking my body.

My body seems to realize that something is wrong while my brain is a muddled mess, just trying to find which way is up.

I become weightless as the darkness wins out.

29

~ Cooper ~

"Calm down before you get arrested," I warn Maverick, stepping out the front door of the police station.

He kicks a trash can, knocking it over onto the curb.

"Get him under control!" Jim, the police chief warns, pointing a finger towards him, holding the door.

Eli stops to right the trash can, nodding at Jim before jogging behind us.

Maverick hops into the passenger seat, slamming the car door behind him.

"A bunch of hillbilly shitheads! Don't even know how to do their jobs." He growls as I start the car.

Kai and Eli climb into the back, smartly staying silent.

"We'll figure something out." I try to placate him.

"Figure what out? Even with everything he just said, they won't hold him. They're going to let him walk free while we're sitting on evidence of him kidnapping girls. Girls who are still missing because that dumbass lets his officers close the cases!"

I get his frustration; I feel it too.

Six hours in an interrogation room with Beck acting like a smug asshole and talking in circles.

He didn't deny having interacted with the girls, and he had no explanation as to where he went with them when they were seen leaving the back of the bar on the feeds that Charlotte pulled.

Even with his attitude and his obvious involvement that only came across as suspicious, the chief stated that we had no leg to stand on, releasing Beck and sending us on our way.

Something wasn't adding up.

The sheriff at JSO thought we had solid grounds for suspecting Beck, and we knew that was right after Kai and Eli filled us in on their little adventure the other day, and what Charlotte found on his computer.

We just couldn't use that as evidence right now.

But they were too quick to dismiss our concerns today. From the moment we got there, everyone acted like it was all a waste of time.

"I know, but we know what we have on him. We just need to get creative now that we don't have the cops on our side."

"Charlotte's already running herself into the ground. We tell her that this went to shit and it's only going to get worse."

She is going to be devastated.

But we'll have to deal with that as it comes.

We can't tear her away from this case, but we will have to keep a closer eye on her to make sure she isn't drowning herself in work and overwhelming herself.

Everything was going to shit.

We needed to take a step back and just recoup. Really take our time to come up with a plan on what to do next.

Don't jump into things without thinking them through. Like the three of them did just a few days ago.

Maverick and I were pissed when they told us about breaking into the bar.

Logically, I understand why they decided to do it. But it was reckless and stupid, and they should've called us before just jumping into it.

We arrive back at the hotel, drained and ready to just see Charlotte and collect ourselves.

The room is silent when we make it back. I'm a little shocked that she's not awake and back at her computer, looking for her next lead.

I look for some takeout menus while Kai heads towards her room to check on her.

He steps back out only moments later.

“Is Lottie in one of your rooms?” He asks, already heading towards Eli’s room, throwing the door open, and turning back around when he comes up empty.

Maverick storms across the living room, flinging both his and my door open.

“Charlotte?”

Instantly on edge, ice fills my veins.

Searching every room and bathroom in the suite, we all come up empty.

Standing in the living room, dumbfounded, Eli pulls his phone out, holding it to his ear.

I hear something vibrating. Stepping over to her desk, I find her phone on the table, Eli’s face filling the screen.

“Her phone’s here,” I tell them.

“Where the fuck is she?” Maverick is furious, seething like a bull; he looks around as if she’ll magically appear.

“I’ll go check the gym,” Kai offers, rushing from the room.

“Do you think she left to get food or something?” The doubt in my voice is audible even to my own ears.

“She wouldn’t leave without her phone. She doesn’t go anywhere without it.”

Maverick doubles over, chest heaving, and his hands fisting his hair.

Grabbing his shoulder, I lead him to the couch before he falls over. Trying to keep him together.

"I can't do this again." He gasps, clutching his chest. "We lost her once; I can't lose her again."

Pushing his head down between his knees, I direct him to breathe.

He's having a panic attack.

"We don't know that she's gone, let's just take a second." My words fall on deaf ears, his breathing becomes more erratic, and he just keeps repeating himself.

Eli paces the room behind me, beginning to panic as well.

I feel my own heart pounding in my chest, threatening to jump right out of my chest.

Kai walks back in, his face ashen. His eyes are void of any emotion, and he stares off into space, looking at nothing.

"She wasn't in the gym." He admits what I already guessed.

The sound that comes from Maverick doesn't even sound human. Somewhere between a growl and a cry.

"Where is she?" Eli asks.

None of us has an answer.

30

~ Charlotte ~

My throat feels like sandpaper, and my head pounds.

The pressure in my head makes me want to gouge my own eyes out just to relieve the pressure.

Something cold and hard presses into my cheek, smelling of dirt.

Blinking, I slam my eyes shut when they're assaulted by the blinding light in the room.

Did I fall asleep with the blinds open?

I manage to open them, having to squint while my eyes adjust.

I find my glasses lying beside me.

Slipping them on, I still, taking in the room around me.

I'm no longer in my bed at the hotel.

The room around me is made of concrete. No larger than eight feet in either direction.

There's a plastic mat pushed against one wall and a steel bucket against the other.

A bottle of water sits by the door, unopened.

Dragging myself off the floor takes all my effort. My legs tremble beneath me like a newborn fawn.

Grabbing the door handle, I try to push it open, feeling my hands begin to shake when I find it locked.

I feel my chest begin to cave in as I struggle to breathe. Panic flooding through me, taking hold of me and wrapping around my lungs like a vise.

Looking around the room, I find no other exits. Not even a window.

I try to rationalize this. To piece together how I ended up here, but I come up blank.

The last thing I remember was falling asleep after the guys left for the police station.

My neck is sore, reminding me of a faint memory of something pinching me.

I thought I was dreaming at the time, but it's becoming glaringly obvious that I wasn't now.

My legs give out, sending me crashing into the wall, sliding down to the floor.

My eyes begin to darken. Tunnel vision is taking over as I suffocate. Not able to coach myself to breathe.

The door swings open, narrowly missing me.

I could just make out a pair of black boots before I was roughly pulled up by the arm.

"Don't pass out on us yet, sweetheart. The fun's just getting started."

The voice is unfamiliar, deep, and raspy like a chain smoker.

The face that stares back at me is a stranger.

Dark skin, wrinkled by too much time in the sun. A full beard, standing in all directions, the dark color peppered by silver strands.

He pulls me out of the room, my feet dragging uselessly on the concrete under me.

My vision is still blurred by the dark edges, preventing me from seeing my surroundings.

I can only focus on gasping for air and the pain radiating down my arm from his grasp.

He enters another room, slamming me into a chair, tying my wrists and ankles to the arms and legs.

I'm powerless to fight it. And only seconds pass by before I'm completely trapped.

Muffled voices sound around me.

A cold wave of water is thrown over me, drenching me from head to toe.

The shock of the water is enough to make me drag in a lung full of air. My chest still burning.

I blink, clearing some of the water from my eyes.

There are still droplets stuck to the lenses of my glasses, distracting me as I take a look around the room.

This room is also made of concrete, but painted an eggshell white and equipped with a window overlooking treetops and a desk.

An older man sits behind the desk, eyeing me.

Donned in a suit and tattoos over both his hands, he watches me.

He's younger than the man who brought me in here.

Not as wrinkled, and no facial hair.

His blond hair looks shiny under the lights overhead, and his piercing eyes look almost black, reminding me of a snake.

"Well, hello Charlotte," He greets me, sounding anything but welcoming.

"I'd say it's a pleasure to meet you, but you've proven to be quite a thorn in my side, I'm afraid."

"W-w-who are y-y-y-" I try to force words out, but between my stutter and chattering teeth, it's damn near impossible.

He raises a hand.

"I'll save you the trouble, dear. Who I am isn't important; what is important, however, is that I'm a man with a lot of power, and you've seemed to stick your nose where it doesn't belong."

I scan through my brain, looking for anything that can identify the man before me.

Nothing about him is familiar, and I'm fairly certain I've never seen him before.

"You see, I run a very big business, very intricate. And when people start poling around in my business, things get messy." Narrowing his eyes at me, his face hardens.

"I don't like mess."

Fixing his cuff links, he looks completely unaffected.

"When little *rats*, like you, start creating suspicion with some of my girls, it makes things much more complicated for me. And then I lose money when the threat of the cops sniffing around becomes higher."

Girls.

Like Ivy and Valerie.

I thought Beck was the one behind their disappearance, but was he just one piece of the puzzle?

A wave of nausea slams into me. My stomach rolls, and if I had anything in it, I'd be puking yet again.

"I thought long and hard about what to do with you. I figured I'd give you an easy out; you seem like an innocent girl." Standing, he rounds the desk. Leaning against it, he crosses his arms, looking down at me.

"So I sent one of my guys to *take care of you.* But he was obviously incapable of completing the job when one of your little boyfriends came to your rescue."

Flashes of the masked man appear in my mind. I can still feel his hands around my neck, phantom pains from the injuries he inflicted.

"When he failed to do his job, I decided to leave it alone, figuring you would come to your senses and just leave it alone. Obviously, since we're here, you did the opposite of that."

Leaning forward, he places a hand on either arm of the chair, his face inches from mine.

"You should've left if alone. Let the girls go missing and move on with your life."

His cheek brushes mine, and I recoil from his touch.

His hand darts up, gripping my jaw in a punishing grasp, angling my head back so I'm forced to look at him.

"So now I have to decide what to do with you."

Tilting his head, his thumb begins to stroke my cheek, studying my face and taking a quick appraisal of my body.

"I figure I can get a high enough price out of you to make up for all the trouble you've caused."

Yanking my jaw from his grasp, my fight or flight kicks in.

Using every ounce of strength, I struggle against the binds holding me in the chair.

Feeling the sting as the rope cuts into my wrists, blood beginning to slip down around the edges, dripping onto the floor.

“I love when they fight,” He tells no one in particular, standing back and watching my hopeless attempts to get free.

Slumping in the chair, panting from my fight, I hang my head in defeat.

The door creaks behind me, footsteps sounding as someone else enters the room.

“Ah, bossman. Here to check out our latest product?”

I keep my gaze locked on the dirty floor, studying the way my blood stands out against the dull, grey concrete.

I don’t have any desire to look at another one of the monsters planning to sell me.

“I’m afraid we’ve already met.” The new voice answers.

Something about the voice is familiar, forcing me to look up and see who it is.

Stunned into silence, I feel my heart being ripped from my chest.

“D-d-dad?”

“Hello, Charlotte.”

To be continued…

Golden Locke Security Book 3

Coming soon…

Afterword

Oh. My. Goodness.

Another book with Charlotte and her men! I'm so excited to have continued this story, and I couldn't be happier with how they've progressed.

This was such a fun book to write. There were a lot of sleepless nights, but they were so worth it to be able to continue Lottie's story.

I cannot wait to see what happens next and to share it with you all in the grand finale!

A lot of changes happened in my life while I was writing this book, and I'm happy to announce that I'm expecting my baby girl in just a few months!

I'm already working on the final book in Lottie's story, and I will do my best to get it to you as soon as possible while I juggle being a first-time mom.

If you came back from my first book, I just want to take a moment to say thank you! All of the love and support I've gotten since last year has been amazing, and I'm so grateful to each and every one of you who took a chance on a self-published indie author.

I hope you enjoyed the book, and I'd love to hear your feedback!

Come find me on social media and let's talk about it!

Until next time,

B. Lynn Hedge

About the Author

B. Lynn Hedge is a wife and 9-5 worker by day, and a writer by night. She runs on Diet Coke, energy drinks, and power naps.

Born and raised in Florida, she still resides there with her husband and fur babies.

Finishing her debut novel last year, and has published two more books including this continuation of the Golden Locke Series.

Her extensive book collection showcases her favorite genre, romance, and has everything from YA to the darkest of dark romances.

More about B. Lynn Hedge and her upcoming works can be found on social media!

Instagram

TikTok

Facebook Group

www.ingramcontent.com/pod-product-compliance
Lightning Source LLC
LaVergne TN
LVHW100517110826
845146LV00002B/679

* 9 7 9 8 2 3 4 0 4 9 0 4 9 *